BOBCAT AND OTHER STORIES

▼ ▼ ▼

ALSO BY REBECCA LEE

The City Is a Rising Tide

Bobcat

& OTHER STORIES

▼ ▼ ▼

Rebecca Lee

ALGONQUIN BOOKS OF CHAPEL HILL   2013

Published by
ALGONQUIN BOOKS OF CHAPEL HILL
Post Office Box 2225
Chapel Hill, North Carolina 27515-2225

a division of
WORKMAN PUBLISHING
225 Varick Street
New York, New York 10014

"At North Farm" from *A Wave* by John Ashbery. Copyright © 1981, 1982, 1983, 1984 by John Ashbery. Reprinted by permission of Georges Borchardt, Inc., on behalf of the author.

Some of these stories appeared first elsewhere: "Bobcat" was published as a chapbook with Madras Press, 2010; "The Banks of the Vistula" was first published in the *Atlantic Monthly,* 1997; "Slatland" was first published in the *Atlantic Monthly,* 1992; "Min" was first published in the *Atlantic Monthly,* 1995; "Fialta" was first published in *Zoetrope,* 2000.

This is a work of fiction. While, as in all fiction, the literary perceptions and insights are based on experience, all names, characters, places, and incidents either are products of the author's imagination or are used fictitiously.

LIBRARY OF CONGRESS CATALOGING-IN-PUBLICATION DATA
    Lee, Rebecca, [date]
        [Short stories. Selections]
        Bobcat and other stories / by Rebecca Lee.—First edition.
            pages cm
        ISBN 978-1-61620-173-9
        1. Short stories, American.   2. American fiction.   I. Title.
    PS3612.E348525B63 2013
    C813'.6—dc23   2013001869

10 9 8 7 6 5 4 3 2 1
First Edition

Somewhere someone is traveling furiously toward you,
At incredible speed, traveling day and night,
Through blizzards and desert heat, across torrents, through
Narrow passes.
But will he know where to find you,
Recognize you when he sees you,
Give you the thing he has for you?

— JOHN ASHBERY

CONTENTS

▼ ▼ ▼

BOBCAT AND OTHER STORIES
▼ ▼ ▼

BOBCAT

▼ ▼ ▼

It was the terrine that got to me. I felt queasy enough that I had to sit in the living room and narrate to my husband what was the brutal list of tasks that would result in a terrine: devein, declaw, decimate the sea and other animals, eventually emulsifying them into a paste which could then be riven with whole vegetables. It was like describing to somebody how to paint a Monet, how to turn the beauty of the earth into a blurry, intoxicating swirl, like something seen through the eyes of the dying. Since we were such disorganized hosts, we were doing a recipe from *Food and Wine* called the quick-start terrine. A terrine rightfully should be made over the course of two or three days—heated, cooled, flagellated, changed over time in the flames of the ever-turning world, but our guests were due to arrive within the hour.

Of the evening's guests, I was most worried about the Donner-Nilsons, whom my husband called the Donner-Blitzens. I had invited them about a month ago, before it had begun to dawn on me that one-half of the couple—Ray Nilson—was having an affair with a paralegal at work, a paralegal so beautiful it was hard to form any other opinions of her. I suppose Ray felt in her presence something that seemed to him so original that he had to pay attention even if he had a wife and a small baby at home.

My friend Lizbet was also coming, and I had filled her in on the situation, making her promise that she would reveal nothing at the dinner, even with her eyes. "My eyes?" she had said, innocently. Lizbet was so irrepressible that I could imagine her raising her eyebrows very slowly for Ray's wife, darting them suddenly over to Ray. *Watch out!*

Lizbet was the person who had introduced me to my husband, John. She and I had been children together, and then during the years I was getting a law degree at NYU, she and John had been writing students together in the state of Iowa. This fall, ten years after they'd graduated, both had novels being published. Lizbet's was about the search for the lost Gnostic Gospel texts, and the book was already, prepublication, being marketed as the thinking woman's *The Da Vinci Code*. My husband's book was a

There is an incomplete line at the end of the first full paragraph on page 5. The sentence should end as follows:

. . . and then the narrator's true love was a sexy Burmarian/Iranian waif named Zita.

The publisher regrets the error.

novel about a war correspondent getting traumatized in some made-up Middle Eastern country that sounded a lot like Iran but was named Burmar in the book.

Truthfully, I was not pleased with his book. I had just finished reading it for the first time, in galleys, and within the first forty pages, the protagonist had slept with three women, none of whom even remotely resembled me—one was an aging countess, another a midwestern farm-girl TV journalist, and then the narrator's true love was a

"Who is Zita?" I had asked him early this afternoon. I was hovering over a roast, trying to figure out how to tie it for the oven.

"She's nobody," he said. He was carrying into our apartment bags of groceries and he leaned over to kiss my cheek.

"Who is she, though?"

"She's a fictional character."

"Do you think our unborn child will one day want to read about your sexual fantasies of other women in war zones?"

"Wait," he said. His head was cocked to the side, as it was when he felt confused or hurt and wanted to explain something. He looked innocent, yet interested. "First," he said, "there is no Zita. Secondly, the protagonist in the book is not me."

"Zita is Frances," I said. It was absurd, I knew. Frances was Frances Sofitel, his book editor, who was also due to show up at our house in a few hours for this dinner party, a woman as unlike a waif as humanly possible. She was tall and very angular, and spoke with an authoritative baritone, and seemed always properly amused by all the underlings around her. As well, she actually managed to make quite a bit of money as an editor, partly by digging in the muck a little, a celebrity bio here, a porn star's memoir there, just a little bit on the side to allow her to publish what she considered her heart and soul, books like my husband's literary thriller and paean to women who weren't his wife.

She and my husband had what I thought was an overly intimate connection. I didn't really like to see them together. They actually talked about language itself a lot. Just words and puns and little synonyms and such. This was completely dull to me, which in addition to my jealousy was a terrible combination. For instance, we would all be out to dinner, and one of them would dig out a little piece of paper so they could play an acrostic, or dream a little about sentences that were the same backwards as forwards. For my husband, words were fascinating—their origins and mutations, their ability to combine intricately. When somebody would say something in an economical way, and use grammar originally to some satisfying end, he would usually repeat it to me at the end of the day. It stayed in his mind, like a song or a painting he loved. I did feel he would be a very good father, partially for this reason, as I could already picture him crouched over the baby, listening, rapt, waiting for the words to come in.

"Zita is not Frances, nor is she any woman," he said. "It's fiction."

"You spend all your time writing, so we'd have to say that those women take up the lion's share of your time—they are your significant others."

"Well, then, we'd have to say that Duong Tran is your significant other," John said. Duong Tran was a Hmong immigrant who had refused to give his dying wife treatment for her heart condition on account of the medication being, according to Duong, Western voodoo and not ordained by the many gods who'd traveled alongside them from Laos to New York City in July of 2001. I was his lawyer.

The argument devolved from there. Certain themes got repeated—John's intense solitude, my long hours, his initial resistance to commitment, my later resistance to marriage, and then at some point the reasons were left behind and we were in that state of pure, extrarational opposition.

Our argument was both constrained and exacerbated by the fact that I was pregnant and had read that high levels of cortisol in a troubled mother can cross the placenta and not only stress out the baby in utero but for *the rest of its life*. As well, there was a deadline; our dinner party was set to begin. People were soon going to be out in the streets and on the subway, making their way to our apartment. They wouldn't want to picture their hostess like this—emotional, insecure, lashing out at her husband. You want the hostess to be serene, the apartment a set of glowing rooms awaiting you, quiet music pouring out of its walls, the food making its way through various complex stages in the kitchen—the slow broiling fig sauce, the buns in the warming oven, the pudding forming its subtle skin in the chill of the refrigerator.

Lizbet arrived early. She helped me hoist myself up from the couch and then stood in the bathroom with me while I put on my makeup. Lizbet was a very spiritual person whose gifts of the spirit—patience, warmth, wonder— were quite available to her friends. Though her novel was about the Gnostic Gospels, her personal life was governed by the slightly spooky, semi-Christian ideas in the book *A Course in Miracles,* which was written by two Columbia psychology professors in 1976, both of whom believed that they were channeling the voice of Jesus, though a Jesus in- flected with a kind of cool, Buddhist gravitas.

Lizbet had brought a huge trifle for dessert, and it stood gleaming on the kitchen counter in an enormous glass bowl. Normally I didn't really like trifle—its layers of bright, childish tastes; strawberry, coconut, sugar. But Lizbet's trifle was perfect and mysterious-seeming—anise, raspberry, and port, with a gingerbread base. Lizbet basi- cally knew how to live a happy life and this was revealed in the trifle—she put in what she loved and left out what she didn't. Her novel was the same really—a collection of treasures, a pleasure-taking, a finding of everything praise-worthy and putting it into words, with one concession to the traditional plot at its heart, which was the death of an important Gnostic scholar at the hands of his former student—a radical feminist—whom he had sexually harassed in college. What could be better?

Standing in front of the mirror, it occurred to me that Lizbet and I were living out our mothers' dreams for us—mine that I finally be pregnant and Lizbet's mother's that she never be pregnant. Our mothers had met in a consciousness-raising group in late 1967, in the East Village. They had become best friends, even though Lizbet's mother was a radical feminist, even a lesbian separatist for a while, without ever working up to actually sleeping with other women, and my own mother liked feminism only as a sort of hobby, a way to chat with a big, cozy group of women eating coffee cakes. Once she told me that feminism had given her some good "tips" for dealing with husbands, such as, *Don't cry; resist.* My mother had moved to Boston when she was pregnant with me and set up my beautiful childhood home, ablaze with light and happiness, the seasons passing through it effortlessly—pumpkin muffins, the deep winter solstice, the return of spring, and then the whole house flung open all summer, more and more babies arriving over the years.

Lizbet lived with her mother in the Village, and as I grew older I traveled by train to see her as many weekends as I could. Their tiny apartment always seemed like a great bohemian experiment to me, a little jerry-rigged maybe, but ultimately exciting — with its hanging wicker chair and its profusion of plants, the total devotion in that home to interesting, liberating ideas. Lizbet's mother was a campus radical at NYU, a clever Andrea Dworkin–style feminist, whose mind seemed a reservoir of interesting, possibly in-correct beliefs, which nevertheless were powerful enough to transform the culture. She *tried out* ideas. She taught Lizbet that ideas were tools to excavate the truth, not the truth itself, which lies somewhat beyond the reach of minds, so to be in their house was like being in the middle of a never-ending, fascinating conversation at all times.

THEN CAME SUSAN. SHE had also published a book, also with Frances as editor, about a near-fatal tussle she'd had with a bobcat while scaling a small mountain in Nepal. The memoir had been out for a year and I was ashamed that I hadn't read it yet, especially as she was coming to our apartment for dinner. Earlier in the day I had gone online and read some reviews, hoping I could fake my way through.

She appeared at our door with a big armful of flowers and some bread she had baked herself. Her left arm had been torn up by the bobcat and later amputated, so that one sleeve fell empty. She had very blond hair and was a large, athletic woman with a wide, peaceful, Swedish-type face.

Frances appeared right behind Susan, dark to Susan's light, talking and cerebral to Susan's calm and silence. Susan at first seemed more of a presence than a personality. It struck me as interesting that she'd battled with an animal because she seemed so much like a certain type of large animal herself—serene, economical, introverted, with none of the neurosis a normal person has buzzing off them at every second.

We all settled into the living room. Lizbet immediately turned to Susan and told her how much she admired her memoir. And then she asked her what took her to Nepal and her fateful encounter with the bobcat.

"Well," Susan said. She settled deeply into our couch: it surrounded her cozily. "It was a strange time in my life. I was engaged to be married and I realized, quite suddenly, that I didn't want any of it. I didn't want to plan a wedding shower, I didn't want to buy a house together, I didn't want to join my bank account with his. I was reading Joseph Campbell, the Sufis, Margaret Mead, and I started thinking, where is my ecstasy? I mean, where is it? Where is ecstasy, where is bliss, or even just fulfillment? Where is it?" She was looking intently at each of us. But we were in the first minutes of meeting her, and I felt unprepared to be plunged into life's deepest questions.

"I just didn't want any of it," Susan said. "I mean, what is marriage? What is it?"

Frances startled and reached into her purse to pull out

her trembling cell phone. She peered into its tiny screen and then she darted up from the table and out to the balcony to answer.

Meanwhile, Susan looked carefully into each of our faces. She was actually waiting for us to answer, to give reasons why people fall in love and get married.

Nobody knows, I wanted to say. Nobody really knows. But that doesn't mean you're allowed to not do it.

DING-DONG. I TOOK A deep breath. The Donner-Nilsons were here. Kitty Donner came in first, looking pretty in her pale, reserved way. I was ashamed that immediately I compared her to the paralegal, whose looks were almost insanely good. Certainly this was another problem—though secondary—with your husband having an affair like this; everybody would constantly be comparing you to this other woman. Kitty was actually a formidable and special person—she was intelligent and watchful, she had a real empathy about her that made her connect quietly but nearly instantly with people; you could trust her to take your side. At the office, sitting in our sterile conference room where we daily and nightly worked out Duong Tran's fate, I generally thought of Ray in a somewhat holistic way, as a brilliant legal strategist and funny colleague—a crowd-pleaser, really—an essentially good-hearted man with an unfortunate personal problem on his hands, but now, tonight, walking behind his wife in her strange, boxy, black-and-red kimono dress down our tiny entrance hallway, it became clear that he was simply a cheater; it was just basic and stupid. What felt to him to be a genuine and essential stirring, a deep response to beauty, was really just life having its way with him. If one of the things people do is establish a civilization out of nature, a way out of the chaos, then Ray was failing at being a person, falling back into the glut of the physical world. He'd been fooled by life. It had triumphed over him. I wanted to call it out to him, over his wife's head, *Hey Ray, life has triumphed over you.*

I was interpreting each of Kitty's movements through the lens of what a woman does who perhaps senses but doesn't yet know her husband is having an affair. But she was a tentative woman anyway, so it was hard to say what she knew or didn't know. I had always found her sort of moving, actually, as it was possible to see her perpetually struggling to move past her hesitation. She sat down a little awkwardly since her kimono dress came open both at the neck and at the legs, but while she was rearranging herself, she looked at me and also put her hand on her stomach. "Oh I forgot about your baby," she said. "It's wonderful; there's so much in store for you."

John came in from the kitchen with the terrine, which looked, perhaps, not great. A terrine really does need to be great to be not awful—it is meant to evince a perfect melding of disparate entities—the lion lying with the lamb, the sea greeting the land, and so forth. John placed it on the coffee table and looked at me worriedly. I saw a flicker of alarm cross Kitty's face. Once John and I had been at a dinner party in Manhattan and the hostess had served us an opening dish of fox meat, so I knew how Kitty felt. (Later that night John had quoted the beautiful Jane Kenyon poem as we drove home along the FDR — *Let the fox go back to its sandy den. Let the wind die down. Let the shed go black inside.*)

As John began passing out little dishes for the hors d'oeuvres, I turned to Kitty and said, "We're not prepared at all. We just found out yesterday at our Lamaze class that we're supposed to have a theme for our nursery."

"Theme?" Lizbet said. "What do you mean, theme? Like man vs. nature?"

"How about alienation in the technological age?" Ray said.

"Hollywood under McCarthy?" Lizbet said.

"It's going to be Winnie the Pooh," John said, which was true. Everybody seemed a bit dejected that John was closing down the joke so early, but he made a recovery. "Winnie the Pooh and the Reconstructed South," he said. And then suddenly Frances out on the balcony was rapping on the glass door, making big surprised eyes at John, the sort of look that I've only seen wives make at their own husbands. John went to the door and conferred with her in whispers.

And then he returned to our guests, apologizing. "You'll

have to forgive my editor for skipping the appetizers; there is a Salman Rushdie proposal floating around the city today, to various editors, and she is trying to get a copy of it sent here tonight."

"A novel?" I asked.

"Memoir," he said. "About the fatwa."

"No kidding," said Lizbet. "There's a book you'd want to read."

Everybody's minds filled with it—Salman as a small child running along the banks of the Ganges, rising as a student at Oxford, ascending as a literary star in England, and then the terrible fatwa raining down, followed by years in hiding. I had seen him give a reading at an ACLU conference in Atlanta soon after 9/11. The person introducing him had said, to a very hushed, still shell-shocked crowd, "We are all Salman now."

I HAD INJECTED THE roast with an infusion of rosemary, palm and olive oils, and a nutty oil made from macadamias. It was an experiment. The infusion had gone in via needle, before the roast took its place in the oven, hunkered in during the whole harrowing argument, safe as a little lamb from its fighting parents.

And as we now pulled it out, an oaky, forest-floor smell filled the kitchen. "The beast emerges," John said. One thing I loved about John's novel, beneath all my possibly irrational rage about the female characters, was his romantic, bohemian ideas about life's pleasures—food, trees, words, gestures. His mother was from a long line of extremely cultivated East Coast women, mostly all living in Manhattan, who used their wealth and privilege as a means to appreciate life. At our wedding, John's aunt had read a Rilke poem, which included those famous lines about marriage—that in it "two solitudes protect and greet each other." It had seemed almost comical to me at the time, that that could possibly be what a family was, a "shelter for the soul's independence." I knew it as a big, semiangry group of people griping at and with each other continually, though in a way that could seem life affirming. In my experience, you would no more expect to find peace within a family than you would expect to find it in yourself.

Our marriage was happy, I believed, though there were some puzzles in it, one of which occurred almost immediately. Our honeymoon had been at a place in Ireland called County Clanagh. The first day we were there we went out sightseeing, and while I placed a call back home from the car, John went out walking. When I emerged, I saw him crouched down in the middle of a field. This field grew out of not dirt, but pebbles really. It surprised me that anything could grow out of those stones, but there was a bright-green grass that seemed to be thriving, and a lot of blue-bells. To the left there were great hills, and to our right a cliff that semicircled around us and fell to an enormous angry shoreline, busy with churning. I couldn't imagine why John was kneeling there. "Are you okay?" I shouted into the wind, over the ocean, and then as I picked my way across the rocks, a line from H.D., whom I hadn't read since college, rose up to me, "At least I have the flowers of myself." When I reached John, I touched his shoulder, and when he turned to look at me, he was crying.

I had asked him why, and when he didn't answer, I hadn't ever asked again, a fact that as it turns out I was mistakenly proud of. I felt like I was respecting the mystery of another person, maybe, and that this harsh landscape was the perfect place to learn my first lesson of marriage, an austere little lesson. And yet County Clanagh had haunted our marriage a little, mostly because it was a little sad for reasons I couldn't comprehend and felt I shouldn't disturb.

After John and I had set the food on the table, Frances came in from the balcony and I introduced her to the Donner-Nilsons.

"Donner as in Donner Family?" Frances asked as she shook Kitty's hand.

"Actually, yes," Kitty said.

Frances would find the book in anybody; she would shake it out of a person. "Which of the Donners do you descend from?" Frances asked.

"George and Tamsen," Kitty said.

"Tamsen's my favorite!" I said. I'd seen a ballet about the Donners at the Met in 2001. Tamsen was the great matriarch of the family, losing herself finally in a little lean-to, alongside the vicious Keseberg. They'd been stranded for weeks when the cannibalism set it, yet still Tamsen was so vigorous and organized that she labeled all the flesh in jars, so that family members could avoid their own family.

"There was no cannibalism," Kitty said. She knew what we were all thinking.

"What?" I blurted out. That was the main thing, the cannibalism.

"There's no evidence in the fossil record."

It was sort of disappointing, actually. Apparently the new thinking among some archeologists was that there wasn't enough forensic evidence—knife marks on the bones, essentially—to support a conclusion of cannibalism.

"I still watch myself," Ray said. "I watch my back."

I DID NOT WISH to be one of those "work wives," women who take up with a married coworker and, while not sleeping with him, take on other very wifely duties— keeping track of him throughout the day, establishing inside jokes, noting his food and drink preferences, texting messages *en francais* back and forth all day. But Ray and I had been working on the Tran case so closely for the past four months that it had necessitated spending inordinate amounts of time together, sometimes deep into the night. I had come to rely on Ray's intelligence and good sense of humor. He was in general such a decent guy, very sympathetic to Duong Tran, very funny, very warm, and hard working.

One night, about a month before the dinner party, Ray and I were holed up in our conference room, eating chow mein, trying to find our way through the eye of the needle, that is, making a way for Duong Tran to stay out of jail. Duong was facing a possible twenty years in prison if we went to court, whereas opposing counsel was now offering us a settlement of two years. I couldn't bear to allow Duong to enter prison. He'd already lost his wife and had a two-year-old baby to support. He was a very earnest, very stubborn man, set in his ways, which were somewhat strange. His beliefs sounded bizarre to me, but then again so did my own, if said aloud. Essentially, the Hmong believed that the gods had to be appeased and sometimes this involved offering a living sacrifice in place of a person, to balance out the forces of life and death on earth. And who was I to say what was superstition: I didn't know. In fact, that was my whole legal argument. It's cruel to punish a man for doing what he considered the best on behalf of his wife. All the precedents for this, unfortunately, involve cases of legal insanity and I didn't think it would go well in court to call four centuries of Hmong religious thinking insanity.

I did think people should just leave him alone, and I thought the law should enforce this. He was grief-stricken by the death of his wife. It's true he hadn't given her the beta-blockers and blood pressure medication she had re-quired (and more problematically, had flushed all the medi-cation down the toilet), but Duong had, as a sign of his love and devotion, hauled a squealing seven-year-old pig up the four flights of stairs to their Brooklyn apartment and butchered it right there in front of her.

Ray thought we should settle and I could not agree to it, so we were still working on the case at two a.m., deliri-ous from exhaustion. Adding to the anxiety of the night, Ray's wife kept calling his cell phone, and it would whirr and vibrate on the table periodically, spinning around angrily. I pictured her at home, holding the baby in one arm, throwing down her cell with the other hand when he wouldn't answer.

At some point, we drifted into pure silence, right after Ray said, "Well, I think your decision means he'll go to prison then for the full twenty." And into that silence, there was a little light rapping at the door. I thought it had to be Kitty. We both turned toward it, and then Lakshmi peered her head around the corner. She smiled and held out a little white bag. "Late-night Danish?" she asked.

What the hell was Lakshmi doing here with a little Danish in a bag? I knew what that little Danish meant to them; I had been newly in love once. It was unbelievable that somebody would go to Hammerstein's around the cor-ner and pick out a jelly Danish and bring it out of the night into the harsh incandescence of our offices and hand it to you. It was irresistible, of course, it represented the whole world outside our sterile, deadlocked conference room, the ongoing life of midtown even deep into the middle of the night, its letting on to the East River, which flows south to downtown, where everyone is always free. But get a clue, Ray. Your wife is at home with a baby.

As Ray conferred with Lakshmi in the hallway, I sat inside the room, waiting, growing more furious by the second. The phone rang again, and without really looking, I opened the door and thrust it out toward Ray. "It's your wife," I said, and with my pregnant belly I was better able to represent all the wives and mothers of the world. Lakshmi smiled kindly at me, though, as beautiful as ever, unruffled, happy, in love.

JOHN TOOK TO CUTTING the meat, and Kitty turned to Ray. "Meat, meat, meat, meat, meat, meat, meat, meat, meat, meat," she said, many more times than seemed amusing or rational. At first I had thought she was just being kind of cute, or silly. Maybe just suddenly exuberant? She spent essentially all day every day with her baby so maybe she was only breaking free a little bit amid the adults, without really remembering how, but then as the "meats" continued, her voice revealed a little bit of harshness or even madness in those short syllables. So she knew about Ray and Lakshmi?

A part of her knew, and it was making the rest of her crazy, was my diagnosis. She was going to lose her mind if she said one more "meat." Everybody smiled nervously.

Finally Kitty turned to the rest of us, her eyes brimming with light and tears, and gave us this nonexplanation. "Ray has been reading a book about women and power that says that women's needs for iron, especially during their periods or after childbirth, is the basis of civilization as we know it. Particularly after childbirth, women generally couldn't procure meat, so they had to trust men to do it."

We all nodded, all of us silent and afraid.

"So women were forced to invent civilization, to surround themselves with stability during their weakest moments and the moments of their children's most terrible vulnerability."

"Women invented civilization then?" John said.

"Well, yes. But they invented it through men."

"It sounds like a lot of trouble."

"It was," Kitty said, demurely.

So she knew? This conversation seemed constructed explicitly to torture a cheating husband. Right? She was bereft of the very thing she and her child needed, and he was not fulfilling his duties as a man. But Ray was munching away on my mother's *mince de déjeuner* casserole, a hearty, simple dish whose secret ingredient was Lipton's chicken noodle soup mixed with root vegetables.

"And time, too, we invented time," Kitty said.

At which point Susan leaped into the conversation, lecturing us on time expanding and then constricting when you are losing your limb over the frozen steppes of Nepal. Apparently when blood leaks out of a body, the body loses its pulsing internal clock, and all understanding of time is released. The soul becomes loosed from the body and unhinged from time simultaneously and begins to rove freely about. There is nothing more beautiful, Susan said, than dying. The end is joy. This little lecture briefly distracted us from the Donner-Nilson marital problems, and by the time Susan was done, Kitty was escaping out to the balcony, her whole body hunched forward as if to hide and comfort herself. Somebody had to tell her.

AS THE TABLE STAYED riveted to Susan's recounting of the attack—the bobcat spotting her from hundreds of feet away, stalking her through the foothills, coming upon her kneeling over a small pond, and placing his paw on her shoulder as if to say, politely, *Hello?*—I followed Kitty out to the balcony, where she stood gripping the railing. "I feel fine out here," she said to me. She was staring out over the city, the rain falling softly into it. "I wish I could just stand out here forever."

"Is everything all right?" I said.

"Yes," she said. "It is. I'm just a wreck, though. I should feel so grateful but ever since I had the baby, I've been falling apart. I can't seem to pull myself together."

"I can imagine how a new mother would feel that way," I said.

"I shouldn't be telling you this," she said. "I'm sure it will be different for you."

"Oh no, no, don't worry."

"Every day just seems so empty."

"Is there anything that helps?"

"I guess, yes. Maybe Ray helps a little. But I've been so awful to him. I'm angry all the time, or sad. I just don't know what to do with myself. I'm so sorry," she said, and then stared out at the city.

The city never disappoints, John frequently said when we set out on an excursion, even a tiny one to the drugstore or for a walk around the park. It was true. Kitty and I both looked out at it now—the lights, its long winding roads, the million interiors. It doesn't know what you want so it tries to give you everything. It was October, the most beautiful month of the year, and even in the city tonight, and under a light rain, you could smell the burning—leaves, grass, the earth, everything golden burning up, surrendering before winter arrives. I looked back in at the candlelit table; people were in high spirits, and nobody seemed to mind that two of the women were out weeping on the balcony. Except then I did catch Ray's eye, and he seemed to shrink away a little. Good.

▼ ▼ ▼

"LET'S JUST GO OUT there right now and tell her, in front of him," Lizbet said. She and I were in the kitchen, preparing the trifle, and Kitty was back at the table, tucked up against Ray.

"Don't tell her *now*," I said. "Don't tell her in the middle of the dinner."

"This party is like a torture chamber for her."

I agreed with Lizbet that Kitty needed to know, but I couldn't bear for her to be told right now. "Some women don't want to know," I said. "Who knows what sort of arrangement they have?"

"I'm pretty sure they have a normal arrangement along the lines of not sleeping with other people."

"I suppose. But the dream of a happy family can be so overpowering that people will often put up with a lot to approximate it. Sometimes a little blindness keeps the family together."

"Well, then tear the family to pieces if it requires that."

"I guess, but you know—children and all."

"People need to have fewer children if what they do is just keep us all in lockstep."

"I know," I said. "I used to think about what was happening in, like, Kosovo, but now I'm researching baby gates deep into the night."

"Oh my god. Are you going to get one of those plastic playgrounds in your backyard?"

"Except that I don't have a backyard."

"It's kind of a drag for the rest of us when people have children."

"It's just that you don't want to use your child as a scythe to break through the forest of received opinion."

"That sounds like an okay use of a child," Lizbet said.

None of this was surprising from Lizbet. You could trust her to hold out against any received opinions, as it was sort of the way Lizbet herself was raised. Her mother, Hanna, had gotten pregnant at twenty-seven, by accident. In fact, there was a still an IUD in Hanna's uterus when she discovered she was pregnant, and it was too dangerous to remove it, so Lizbet grew in the womb alongside the little piece of barbed wire, an almost impossibility, and a fact that we were all strangely proud of.

"Anyway," I said, "I'm going to go crazy if I have to listen to Susan anymore."

"She's smart," Lizbet said.

"I don't even believe there was a bobcat."

"What?"

"Seriously. A bobcat isn't really even big enough to tear off a woman's arm. Bobcats are quite cute and little."

"You think she made it up, are you crazy?"

"Made what up?" John said, entering the kitchen.

"The bobcat," I said.

"What?" he said.

"We gotta somehow look up her sleeve," Lizbet said, "and see the type of scar it is."

"You two are crazy. You need to not spend time alone together."

I handed him the huge, chilled trifle and he carried it like a big baby into the dining room, where it was greeted with shouts of happiness.

EVERY DINNER PARTY BY the end is a bit of a defeat. After the halfway mark, when everybody is still in high-spirits, some even intoxicated, and the dessert still hasn't arrived, there is a moment when it seems like we are the most interesting dinner party in Manhattan tonight, we love each other, and we should do this all the time, why don't we do this all the time? Everybody is calculating when they can invite everybody to their house for the next dinner party.

But then there is the subtle shift downward. Somebody is a little too drunk. The bird, which was a bronze talismanic centerpiece, golden and thriving, is revealed as a collection of crazy bones. A single line from the archeologist Ernest Becker often tore through my mind at the end of long meals, that every man stands over a pile of mangled bones and declares life good.

I had learned from my mother, who was an exquisite hostess, that it was important to provide small, gradual treats—little chocolates and liqueurs, after the meal, so that as the night decelerates there is no despair.

There was the trifle, and then fortune cookies, and then John brought in mango.

The alcohol had left Susan nostalgic for the bobcat and her time on the mountain. "What I missed the most," she said, "while I lay there, aware now that my arm would most likely have to be amputated, if I didn't die right there, going in and out of consciousness, what I missed the most was this, the ritual of dinner, the sitting down to sup together."

Oh my god. I looked over at Lizbet and knew she would repeat "sup together" for the rest of our lives.

"It is *written inside us*," Susan said, "to have dinner with our friends. As I crouched down, and he breathed at my back, I went through all the great meals of my life, one by one. The fish at the wharf in my childhood, the beef bourguignon in Falstaff, my grandmother's creampuffs, one by one."

"When you say 'bobcat,'" I said, "are you meaning it metaphorically or actually?"

"Both," Susan said. "I picture it as the fright of your life."

"But when you say 'bobcat' most of us are picturing a really big, ferocious animal."

"And that's fine," she said.

But Frances, as the book's editor, took offense. She sighed and said, bored, "Actually, literature needs to be read as literature, not gone thudding through like one would a law brief."

There was a knock at the door; I leaped up. "That's the Tran decision," I said. I'd asked the night secretary at the firm to bring it over the minute it arrived.

"It'll be the manuscript," Frances said. She said it with such certainty that I half expected a breathless Salman at the door, delivering it himself.

But it was neither, though the Tran case would be settled the next day, with Duong forced to abandon his little boy, and Salman's memoir would get published and it actually would explain our times and it *would* find joy where none previously was. It was just a plain woman at the door, in a long overcoat, asking for my husband. It was such a startling request, and standing there, she formed the perfect answer to the question that was County Clanagh. Unlike the Donner-Nilson marriage, whose dysfunction would turn out to be, deep down, part of its durability—Kitty's solicitude interlocking nicely with Ray's narcissism—our marriage would break apart within months. And when it did, I would understand Susan's book a little better because nothing could describe what was happening, my little boy, just a few months old, already cut loose from the nuclear family—a little spaceman adrift, his parents also cast to the heavens.

Our guests left soon after, leaving behind this woman at

the door, who would stay and stay. I gave the guests some marzipan boats, to eat on the subway, or save for another day. Susan bit into one right away and thanked me for a wonderful party. But she knew. She put her hand on my shoulder, and her eyes let me know, *Just crouch down, hold tight, there's a little bit of pain for you, but not too much.*

THE BANKS
OF THE VISTULA

▼ ▼ ▼

It was dusk; the campus had turned to velvet. I walked the brick path to Humanities, which loomed there and seemed to incline toward me, as God does toward the sinner in the book of Psalms. It was late on a Friday afternoon, when the air is fertile, about to split and reveal its warm fruit—that gold nucleus of time, the weekend. Inside, up the stairs, the door to Stasselova's office was open, and the professor lifted his head. "Oh," he said. "Yes." He coughed, deep in his lungs, and motioned me in. He had requested this visit earlier in the day, following class. His course was titled Speaking in Tongues: Introductory Linguistics. Stasselova was about sixty-five and a big man, his torso an almost perfect square. Behind his balding head the blond architecture of St. Gustav College rose into the cobalt sky. It looked like a rendition of thought itself, rising out of the head in intricate, heartbreaking cornices that became more abstract and complicated as they rose.

I was in my third week of college. I loved every moment of it, every footfall. The students resembled the students I'd known in high school, Scandinavian midwesterners like myself, whose fathers were all pastors or some declension thereof — but the professors thrilled me. Most had come from the East Coast and seemed fragile and miserable in the Midwest. Occasionally during class you could see hope for us rising in them, and then they would look like great birds flying over an uncertain landscape, asking mysterious questions, trying to lead us somewhere we could not yet go.

I wanted to be noticed by them, to distinguish myself from the ordinary mass of students, and to this end I had plagiarized my first paper for Stasselova's class. This was why, I presumed, he had called me to his office.

The paper, titled "The Common Harvest," was on the desk between us. I had found it in the Kierkegaard Library. It was a chapter in an old green-cloth book that was so small I could palm it. The book had been written in 1945 by a man named Delores Tretsky, and it hadn't been signed out since 1956. I began to leaf through it, and then crouched down to read. I read for a full hour; I thought it beautiful. I had not once in all my life stopped for even a moment to consider grammar, to wonder how it rose out of history like a wing unfurling.

I had intended to write my own paper, to synthesize, as Stasselova had suggested, my own ideas with the author's, but I simply had nothing to contribute. It seemed even rude to combine this work with my own pale, unemotional ideas. So I lifted a chapter, only occasionally dimming some passages that were too fine, too blinding.

"THIS IS AN EXTRAORDINARY paper," he said. He was holding his coffee cup over it, and I saw that coffee had already spilled on the page to form a small, murky pond.

"Thank you," I said.

"It seems quite sophisticated. You must not have come here straight out of high school."

"I did," I said.

"Oh. Well, good for you."

"Thanks."

"You seem fully immersed in a study of oppression. Any reason for this?"

"Well, I do live in the world."

"Yes, that's right. And you say here—a shocking line— that a language must sometimes be repressed, and replaced, for the larger good. You believe this?"

"Yes."

"You think that the Eastern-bloc countries should be forced to speak, as you say here, the mother tongue?"

Some parts of the paper I had just copied down verbatim, without really understanding, and now I was stuck with them. Now they were my opinions. "Yes," I said.

"You know I am from that region."

"Is that right?"

"From Poland."

"Whereabouts in Poland?" I asked conversationally.

"I was born on the edge of it, in the dark forest land along its northeastern border, before the Soviet Union took it over completely, burning our towns. As children we were forced to speak Russian, even in our homes, even when we said good night to our mothers as we fell asleep."

This was turning into a little piece of bad luck.

"When did you write this?" he asked.

"Last week."

"It reads like it was written fifty years ago. It reads like Soviet propaganda."

"Oh," I said. "I didn't mean it that way."

"Did somebody help you?"

"Actually, yes. Certainly that's all right?"

"Of course, if done properly. Who was it that helped you, a book or a person?"

"My roommate helped me," I said.

"Your roommate. What is her name?"

"Solveig."

"Solveig what?"

"Solveig Juliusson."

"Is she a linguistics scholar?"

"No, just very bright."

"Maybe I can talk to Solveig myself?"

"Unfortunately, you can't."

"Why not?"

"It's complicated," I said.

"In what way?"

"Well, she's stopped eating. She's very thin. Her parents were worried, so they took her home."

"Where does she live?"

"I don't know."

We both sat silent. Luckily, I had experience lying in my adolescence and knew it was possible to win even though both parties were aware of the lie. The exercise was not a search for truth but rather a test of exterior reserve.

"I'm sure she'll be returning soon," I said. "I'll have her call you."

Stasselova smiled. "Tell her to eat up," he said, his sarcasm curled inside his concern.

"Okay," I said. I got up and hoisted my bag over my shoulder. As I stood, I could see the upper edge of the sun falling down off the hill on which St. Gustav was built. I'd never seen the sun from this angle before, from above as it fell, as it so obviously lit up another part of the world, perhaps even flaming up the sights of Stasselova's precious, oppressed Poland, its dark contested forests and burning cities, its dreamy and violent borders.

MY ROOMMATE SOLVEIG WAS permanently tan. She went twice a week to a tanning salon and bleached her hair frequently, so that it looked like radioactive foliage growing out of dark, moody sands. Despite all this she was very beautiful, and sensible. "Margaret," she said, when I came in that evening. "The library telephoned to recall a book. They said it was urgent."

I had thought he might check the library. "Okay," I said. As I rifled through the clothes on my closet floor, I decided it would have to be burned. I would finish the book and then I would burn it. But first there was tonight, and I had that rare thing, a date.

My date was from Stasselova's class. His name was Hans; he was a junior, and his father was a diplomat. He had almost auburn hair that fell to his neckline. He wore, always, long white shirts whose sleeves were just slightly, almost imperceptibly, puffed at the shoulders, like an elegant little joke, and very long, so they hung over his hands. I thought he was articulate, kind. I had in a moment of astonishment asked him out.

The night was soft and warm. We walked through the tiny town, wandered its thin river. We ate burgers. He spoke of Moscow, where he had lived that summer. I had spent my childhood with a vision of Russia as an anti-America, a sort of fairy-tale intellectual prison. But this was 1987, the beginning of perestroika, of glasnost, and views of Russia were changing. Television showed a country of rain and difficulty and great humility, and Gorbachev was always bowing to sign something or other, his head bearing a mysterious stain shaped like a continent one could almost but not quite identify. I said to Hans that I wanted to go there myself, though I had never thought of the idea before that moment. He said, "You can if you want." We were in his small, iridescent apartment by now. "Or perhaps to Poland," I said, thinking of Stasselova.

"Poland," Hans said. "Yes. What is left of it, after men like Stasselova."

"What do you mean, men like Stasselova?"

"Soviet puppets."

"Yet he is clearly anti-Soviet," I said.

"*Now*, yes. Everybody is anti-Soviet now." The sign for the one Japanese restaurant in town cast a worldly orange light into the room, carving Hans's body into geometric shapes. He took my hand, and at that moment the whole world seemed to have entered his apartment. I found him intelligent, deliberate, large-hearted. "Now," he said, "is the time to be anti-Soviet."

ON MONDAY AFTERNOON, IN class, Hans sat across from me. We were all sitting around a conference table, waiting for Stasselova. Hans smiled. I gave him the peace sign across the table. When I looked back at him, moments later, Hans's hands were casually laid out on the table, palms down. I saw then, for the first time, that his left hand tapered into only three fingers, which were fused together at the top knuckle. The hand looked delicate, surprising. I had not noticed this on our date, and now I wondered if he had purposely kept me from seeing it, or if I had somehow just missed it. For a brief, confused moment, I even wondered if the transformation had occurred between then and now. Hans looked me squarely in the eye. I smiled back. Stasselova then entered the room. In light of my date with Hans, I had almost forgotten my visit with him the previous Friday. I'd meant to burn the book over the weekend in the darkness at the ravine, though I dreaded this. My mother was a librarian, and I knew that the vision of her daughter burning a book would have been like a sledgehammer to the heart.

Throughout the class Stasselova seemed to be speaking directly to me, still chastising me. His eyes kept resting on me disapprovingly. "The reason for the sentence is to express the verb—a change, a *desire*. But the verb cannot stand alone; it needs to be supported, to be realized by a body, and thus the noun—just as the soul in its trajectory through life needs to be comforted by the body."

The sun's rays slanted in on Stasselova as he veered into very interesting territory. "All things in revolution," he said, "in this way, need protection. For instance, when my country, Poland, was annexed by the Soviet Union, we had the choice of joining what was called Berling's Army, the Polish wing of the Russian army, or the independent Home

Army. Many considered it anti-Polish to join the Russian army, but I believed, as did my comrades, that more could be done through the system, within the support of the system, than without."

He looked at me. I nodded. I was one of those students who nod a lot. His eyes were like brown velvet under glass. "This is the power of the sentence," he said. "It acts out this drama of control and subversion. The noun always stands for what is, the status quo, and the verb for what might be, the ideal."

Across the table Hans's damaged hand, spindly and nervy, drummed impatiently on the tabletop. I could tell he wanted to speak up. Stasselova turned to him. "That was the decision I made," he said. "Years ago. Right or wrong, I thought it best at the time. I thought we could do more work for the Polish cause from within the Red Army than from outside it."

Hans's face was impassive. He suddenly looked years older—austere, cold, priestly. Stasselova turned then to look at me. This was obviously an issue for him, I thought, and I nodded as he continued to speak. I really did feel supportive. Whatever army he thought was best at the time, that was fine with me.

IN THE EVENING I went to the ravine in the elm forest, which lay curled around the hill on which the campus was built. This forest seemed deeply peaceful to me, almost conscious. I didn't know the reason for this at the time—that many elms in a forest can spring from a single tree. In this case a single elm had divided herself into a forest, an individual with a continuous DNA in whose midst one could stand and be held. The ravine cut through like an old emotional wound. I crouched on its bank and glanced at the book one last time. I flicked open my lighter. The book caught fire instantly. As the flame approached my hand, I arced the book into the murky water. It looked spectacular, a high wing of flame rising from it. Inside, in one of its luminous chapters, I had read that the ability to use language and the ability to tame fire arose from the same warm, shimmering pool of genes, since in nature they did not appear one without the other.

As I made my way out of the woods and into the long silver ditch that lined the highway, I heard about a thousand birds cry, and I craned my neck to see them lighting out from the tips of the elms. They looked like ideas would if released suddenly from the page and given bodies— shocked at how blood actually felt as it ran through the veins, as it sent them wheeling into the west, wings raking, straining against the requirements of such a physical world.

I RETURNED AND FOUND Solveig turning in the lamplight. Her hair was piled on her head, so unnaturally blond it looked ablaze, and her face was bronze. She looked a thousand years old. "Some guy called," she said. "Stasselova or something."

He called again that night, at nearly midnight. I thought this unseemly.

"So," he said. "Solveig's back."

"Yes," I said, glancing at her. She was at her mirror, performing some ablution on her face. "She's much better."

"Perhaps the three of us can now meet."

"Oh," I said, "it's too early."

"Too early in what?"

"In her recovery." Solveig wheeled her head around to look at me. I smiled, shrugged.

"I think she'll be okay."

"I'm not so sure."

"Listen," he said. "I'll give you a choice: you can either rewrite the paper in my office, bringing in whatever materials you need, or the three of us can meet and clear this up."

"Fine, we'll meet you."

"You know my hours."

"I do." I hung up and explained to Solveig what had happened—Stasselova's obsession with language and oppression, my plagiarism, the invocation of her name. Solveig nodded and said of course, whatever she could do she would.

WHEN WE ARRIVED THAT Wednesday, the light had almost gone from his office but was still lingering outside the windows, like the light in fairy tales, rich and creepy. Solveig was brilliant. Just her posture, as she sat in the narrow chair, was enough initially to chasten Stasselova. In her presence men were driven to politeness, to sincerity, to a kind of deep, internal apology. He thanked her, bowing a little at his desk. "Your work has interested me," he said.

"It is not my work, sir. It's Margaret's. We just discussed together some of the ideas."

"Such as?"

"Well, the necessity of a collective language, a mutual tongue."

"And why is that necessary?" Stasselova leaned back and folded his hands across his vast torso.

"To maintain order," she said. And then the sun fell completely, blowing one last blast of light across the Americas before it settled into the Soviet Union, and some of that light, a glittery, barely perceptible dust, settled around Solveig's head. She looked like a dominatrix, an intellectual dominatrix, delivering this brutal news.

"And your history in psycholinguistics?" he said.

"I have only my personal history," she said. "The things that have happened to me." I would not have been surprised if at that declaration the whole university had imploded, turned to liquid, and flowed away. "Besides," she said, "all the research and work was Margaret's. I saw her working on it, night after night."

"Then, Margaret," he turned his gaze on me, "I see you

are intimately connected with evolutionary history as well as Soviet ideology. As well, it appears, you've been steeped in a lifetime's study of linguistic psychosocial theory."

"Is it because she's female," Solveig asked, "that she's made to account for every scrap of knowledge?"

"Look," he said after a long, cruel silence, "I simply want to know from what cesspool these ideas arose. If you got them from a book, I will be relieved, but if these ideas are still floating around in your bloodlines, in your wretched little towns, I want to know."

I was about to cave in. Better a plagiarist than a fascist from a tainted bloodline.

"I don't really think you should be talking about our bloodlines," Solveig said. "It's probably not appropriate." She enunciated the word "appropriate" in such a way that Stasselova flinched, just slightly. Both he and I stared at her. She really was extraordinarily thin. In a certain light she could look shockingly beautiful, but in another, such as the dim one in Stasselova's office, she could look rather threatening. Her contact lenses were the color of a night sky split by lightning. Her genetic information was almost entirely hidden—the color of her hair and eyes and skin, the shape of her body—and this gave her a psychological advantage of sorts.

STASSELOVA'S LECTURE ON THURSDAY afternoon was another strange little affair, given as long autumn rays of sun, embroidered by leaves, covered his face and body. He was onto his main obsession again, the verb—specifically, the work of the verb in the sentence and how it relates to the work of a man in the world. "The revolution takes place from a position of stability, always. The true revolutionary will find his place within the status quo."

"And this is why you joined the Russian army in attacking your own country?" This was Hans, startling us all.

"I did not attack my own country," Stasselova said. "Never."

"But you watched as the Nazis attacked it in August of 1944, yes? And used that attack for your own purposes?"

"This night I was there, it's true," he said, "on the banks of the Vistula, and I saw Warsaw burn. And I was wearing the fur hat of Russia, yes. But when I attempted to cross the Vistula, in order to help those of my countrymen who were escaping, I was brought down—clubbed with a rifle to the back of the head by my commanding officer, a Russian."

"That's interesting, because in accounts of the time you are referred to as an officer yourself—Officer Stasselova, of course."

"Yes. I was a Polish officer though. Certainly you can infer the hierarchy involved?"

"What I can infer . . ." Hans's voice rose, and then Stasselova's joined in, contrapuntally, "What you can infer . . ." and for a moment the exchange reminded me of those rounds we sang at summer camp. "What you can infer," Stasselova said, drowning out Hans, "is that this was an ambiguous time for those of us who were Polish. You can't judge after the fact. Perhaps you think that I should be dead on those banks, making the willows to grow." Stasselova's eyes were shot with the dying light; he squinted at us and looked out the window momentarily. "You will stand there and think maybe certain men in certain times should not choose their own lives, should not want to live." And then he turned away from Hans. I myself scowled at Hans. So rude!

"And so I did live," Stasselova said finally. "Mostly because I was wearing my Russian hat, made of the fur of ten foxes. It was always Russia that dealt us blows, and it was always Russia that saved us. You see?"

THE NEXT DAY I was with Hans in the woods. We were on our stomachs in a clearing, looking to the east, from where the rain was stalking us through the trees. "What I want to know," Hans was saying, "is why is he always asking for you to see him?"

"Oh," I said, "he thinks I plagiarized that first paper."

"Did you?"

"Not really."

"Why does he think so?"

"Says it smacks of Soviet propaganda."

"Really? Well, he should know."

"I agree with him—that you're judging him from an irrelevant stance."

"He was found guilty of treason by his own people, not me—by the Committee for Political Responsibility. Why else would he be here, teaching at some Lutheran college in Minnesota? This is a guy who brought martial law down on his own people, and now we sit here in the afternoon and watch him march around in front of us, relating everything he speaks of—*comma splices,* for Christ's sake—to his own innocence."

"Yet all sorts of people were found guilty of all sorts of meaningless things by that committee."

"I bet he thinks you're a real dream—this woman willing to absolve the old exterminator of his sins."

"That's insulting," I said. But I realized how fond I'd grown of this professor in his little office, drinking his bitter coffee, night descending into the musky heart of Humanities.

And then the rain was upon us. We could hear it on the tiny ledges of leaves above us more than feel it. "Let's go," Hans said, grabbing my hand with his left, damaged hand. The way his hand held mine was alluring; his hand had the nimbus of an idea about it, as if the gene that had sprung this hand had a different world in mind, a better world, where hands had more torque when they grasped each other, and people held things differently, like hooks—a world where all objects were shaped something like lanterns, and were passed on and on.

MONDAY WAS GRAY, WITH long silver streaks of rain. I dragged myself out of the warmth of my bed and put on my rain slicker. At nine-forty-five I headed toward Stasselova's office. "Hello," I said, knocking on the open door. "I'm sorry to disturb you outside your office hours." I was shivering; I felt pathetic.

"Margaret," he said. "Hello. Come in." As I sat down, he said, "You've brought with you the smell of rain."

He poured me coffee in a Styrofoam cup. During our last class I had been so moved by his description of that night on the Vistula that I'd decided to confess. But now I was hesitating. "Could I have some of this cream?" I asked, pointing to a little tin cup of it on his windowsill.

"There it is again," he said, as he reached for the cream.

"There is what again?"

"That little verbal tic of yours."

"I didn't know I had one," I said.

"I noticed it first in class," he said. "You say 'this' instead of 'that'; 'this cream,' not 'that cream.' The line people draw between the things they consider *this* and the things they consider *that* is the perimeter of their sphere of intimacy. You see? Everything inside is *this;* everything inside is close, is intimate. Since you pointed at the cream and it is farther from you than I am, 'this' suggests that I am among the things you consider close to you. I'm flattered," he said, and handed me the creamer, which was, like him, sweating. What an idea—that with a few words you could catch another person in a little grammatical clutch, arrange the objects of the world such that they bordered the two of you.

"At any rate," he said, "I'm glad you showed up."

"You are?"

"Yes. I've wanted to ask you something."

"Yes?"

"This spring the college will hold its annual symposium on language and politics. I thought you might present your paper. Usually one of the upperclassmen does this, but I thought your paper might be more appropriate."

"I thought you hated my paper."

"I do."

"Oh."

"So you'll do it?"

"I'll think about it," I said.

He nodded and smiled, as if the matter were settled. The rain was suddenly coming down very hard. It was loud, and we were silent for a few moments, listening. I stared beyond his head out the window, which was blurry with water, so that the turrets of the campus looked like a hallucination, like some shadow world looming back there in his unconscious.

"This rain," he said then, in a quiet, astonished voice, and his word *this* entered me as it was meant to—quietly, with a sharp tip, but then, like an arrowhead, widening and widening, until it included the whole landscape around us.

THE RAIN TURNED TO snow, and winter settled on our campus. The face of nature turned away—beautiful and distracted. After Christmas at home (where I received my report card, a tiny slip of paper that seemed to have flown across the snows to deliver me my A in Stasselova's class) I hunkered down in my dorm for the month of January and barely emerged. The dorm in which most of us freshman girls lived was the elaborate, dark Agnes Mellby Hall, named after the stern, formidable virgin whose picture hung over the fireplace in our lounge. As winter crept over us, we retired to Mellby earlier and earlier. Every night that winter, in which most of us were nineteen, was a slumber party in the main sitting room among its ornate furnishings. There, nightly, we ate heavily, like Romans, but childish foods, popcorn and pizza and ice cream, most of us spiraling downstairs now and then to throw up in the one private bathroom.

On one of those nights I was reading a book in the sitting room when I received a phone call from Solveig, who was down at a house party in town and wanted me to come help her home. She wasn't completely drunk but calculated that she would be in about forty-five minutes. Her body was like a tract of nature that she understood perfectly—a constellation whose movement across the night sky she could predict, or a gathering storm, or maybe, more accurately, a sparkling stream of elements into which she introduced alcohol with such careful calibration that her blood flowed exactly as she desired, uphill and down, intersecting precisely, chemically, with time and fertility. Solveig did not stay at the dorm with us much but rather ran with an older pack of girls, feminists mostly, who that winter happened to be involved in a series of protests, romantic insurrections, against the president of the college, who was clearly terrified of them.

About ten minutes before I was to leave, Stasselova appeared in the doorway of the sitting room. I had not seen him in more than a month, since the last day of class, but he had called a few times. I had not returned his calls, in the hopes that he would forget about my participation in the symposium. But here he was, wearing a long gray coat over his bulkiness. His head looked huge, the bones widely spaced, like the architecture of a grand civic building.

The look in his eyes caused me to gaze out across the room and try to see what he was seeing: perhaps some debauched canvas of absolute female repose, girls lying everywhere in various modes of pajamas and sweats, surrounded by vast quantities of food and books. Some girls—and even I found this a bit creepy—had stuffed animals that they carried with them to the sitting room at night. I happened to be poised above the fray, straddling a piano bench, with a book spread in front of me, but almost all the rest were lying on their backs with their extremities cast about, feet propped on the couch or stretched up in the air at weird, hyper extended angles. We were Lutherans, after all, and unlike the more experienced, secular girls across the river, at the state college, we were losing our innocence right here, among ourselves. It was being taken from us physically, and we were just relaxing until it fell away completely.

Stasselova, in spite of all he'd seen in his life, which I'd gleaned from what he said in class (the corpulent Goering marching through the forest, marking off Nazi territory, and later Stalin's horses breaking through the same woods, heralding the swath that would now be Soviet), still managed to look a little scared as he peered into our sitting room, eventually lifting a hand to wave at me.

I got up and approached him. "Hey," I said.

"Hello. How are you, Margaret?"

"It's good to see you. Thanks for the A."

"You deserved it. Listen, I have something for you," he said, mildly gesturing for us to leave the doorway, because everybody was looking at us.

"Great," I said. "But you know, right now I need to walk downtown to pick up Solveig at a house party."

"Fine," he said. "I'll walk you."

"Oh. Okay."

I got my jacket, and the two of us stepped into the night. The snow had arranged itself in curling waves on the Mellby lawn, and stuck in it were hundreds of silver forks, which, in a flood of early-evening testosterone, the freshman boys had placed in the earth, a gesture appropriate to their sexual frustration and also to their faith in the future. Stasselova and I stepped between them. They looked spooky and lovely, like tiny silver gravesites in the snow. As we walked across campus, Stasselova produced a golden brochure from his pocket and handed it to me. On the front it said, in emerald-green letters, "Ninth Annual Symposium on Language and Politics." Inside, under "Keynote Student Speaker," was my name. "Margaret Olafson, 'The Common Harvest.' " I stopped walking. We paused at the top of the stairs that floated down off the campus and into the town. I felt extremely, inordinately proud. Some winter lightning, a couple of great wings of it, flashed in the north. Stasselova looked paternal, grand.

THE AIR AT THE party was beery and wildish, and the house itself—its many random rooms and slanting floors—seemed the product of a drunken adolescent mind. At first we could not spot Solveig, so Stasselova and I waited quietly in the hallway until a guy in a baseball cap came lurching toward us, shouting in a friendly way over the music that we could buy plastic glasses for the keg for two dollars apiece. Stasselova paid him and then threaded through the crowd, gracefully for such a large man, to stand in the keg line. I watched him as he patiently stood there, the snowflakes melting on his dark shoulders. And then Hans was on my arm. "What on earth?" he said. "Why are you here? I thought you hated these parties."

He'd been dancing, apparently. He was soaked in sweat, his hair curling up at his neck.

I pointed to Stasselova.

"No kidding," Hans said.

"He showed up at my dorm as I was leaving to get Solveig."

"He came to Mellby?"

"Yes."

"God, look at him. I bet they had a nickname for him, like the Circus Man or something. All those old fascists had cheery nicknames."

Stasselova was now walking toward us. Behind him the picture window revealed a nearly black sky, with pretty crystalline stars around. He looked like a dream one might have in childhood. "He is not a fascist," I said quietly.

"Professor!" Hans raised his glass.

"Hans, yes, how are you? This is a wonderful party," Stasselova said, and it actually was. Sometimes these parties could seem deeply cozy, their wildness and noise an affirmation against the formless white midwestern winter surrounding us.

He handed me a beer. "So," he said rather formally, lifting his glass. "To youth."

"To experience," Hans said, smiling, and lifted his glass.

"To the party." Stasselova looked pleased, his eyes shining from the soft lamplight.

"The Party?" Hans raised an eyebrow.

"This party," Stasselova said forcefully, cheerfully.

"And to the committee," Hans said.

"The committee?"

"The Committee for Political Responsibility."

In one of Stasselova's lectures he had taken great pains to explain to us that language did not describe events, it handled them, as a hand handles an object, and that in this way language made the world happen under its supervision. I could see that Hans had taken this to heart and was making lurching attempts in this direction.

Mercifully, Solveig appeared. Her drunkenness and her dignity had synergized into something quite spectacular, an inner recklessness accompanied by great external restraint. Her hair looked the color of heat—bright white. She was wearing newly cut-off jeans and was absently holding the disassociated pant legs in her hand.

"The professor," she said, when she saw Stasselova. "The professor of oppression."

"Hello, Solveig."

"So you came," she said, as if this had been the plan all along.

"Yes. It's nice to see you again."

"You as well," she said. "Why are you here?"

The whole scene looked deeply romantic to me. "To take you home," he said.

"Home?" she said, as if this were the most elegant and promising word in the language. "Yours or mine?"

"Yours, of course. Yours and Margaret's."

"Where is your home again?" she asked. Her eyes were glimmering with complexity, like something that is given to human beings after evolution, as a gift.

"I live downtown," he said.

"No, your real home. Your homeland."

He paused. "I am from Poland," he said finally.

"Then there. Let's go there. I have always wanted to go to Poland."

Stasselova smiled. "Perhaps you would like it there."

"I have always wanted to see Wenceslaus Square."

"Well, that is nearby."

"Excellent. Let us go." And Solveig swung open the front door and walked into the snow in her shorts and T-shirt. I kissed Hans good-bye, and Stasselova and I followed her.

Once outside, Stasselova took off his coat and hung it around Solveig. Underneath his coat he was wearing a dark jacket and a tie. It looked sweet and made me think that if one kept undressing him, darker and darker suits would be found underneath.

Solveig was walking before us on the narrow sidewalk. Above her, on the hill, hovered Humanities—great, intelligent, alight. She reached into the coat pocket and pulled out, to my astonishment, a fur hat. The hat! The wind lifted, and the trees shook off a little of their silver snow. Humanities leaned over us, interested in its loving but secular way. I felt as sure about everything as those archaeologists who discover a single bone and can then hypothesize the entire animal. Solveig placed the hat on her head and turned to vamp for a moment, opening and closing the coat and raising her arms above her head in an exaggerated gesture of beauty. She looked like some stirring, turning simulacrum of communist and capitalist ideas. As she was doing this, we passed by the president's house. It was an old-fashioned house, with high turrets, and had a bizarre modern wing hanging off one end of it. Solveig studied it for a moment as she walked, and then suddenly shouted into the cold night, "Motherfucker!"

Stasselova looked as if he'd been clubbed again in the back of the head, but he kept walking. He pretended that nothing had happened, didn't even turn his head to look at the house, but when I turned to him, I saw his eyes widen and his face stiffen with shock. I said "Oh" quietly and grabbed his hand for a moment to comfort him, to let him know that everything was under control, that this was Minnesota. Look—the president's house is still as dark as death, the moon is still high, the snow sparkling everywhere.

His hand was extraordinarily big. After Hans's hand, which I'd held for the past few months, Stasselova's more ordinary hand felt strange, almost mutant, its five fingers splayed and independent.

THE NEXT NIGHT, IN the cafeteria, over a grisly neon dish called Festival Rice, I told Hans about the hat. "I saw the hat," I said. A freshman across the cafeteria stood just then and shouted, in what was a St. Gustav tradition, *"I want a standing ovation!"* The entire room stood and erupted into wild applause and hooting. Hans and I stood as well, and as we clapped, I leaned over to yell, "He's been telling the truth about that night overlooking Warsaw: I saw the hat he was wearing."

"What does that mean? That means nothing. I have a fur hat."

"No," I said. "It was this big Russian hat. You should have seen it. This big, beautiful Russian hat. Solveig put it on. It saved his life."

Hans didn't even try to object; he just kind of gasped, as if the great gears of logic in his brain could not pass this syllogism through. We were still standing, clapping, applauding. I couldn't help thinking of something Stasselova had said in class: that at rallies for Stalin, when he spoke to crowds over loudspeakers, one could be shot for being the first to stop clapping.

I AVOIDED MY PAPER for the next month or so, until spring crashed in huge warm waves and I finally sought it out, sunk in its darkened drawer. It was a horrible surprise. I was not any more of a scholar, of course, than I had been six months earlier, when I'd plagiarized it, but my eyes had now passed over Marx and a biography of Stalin (microphones lodged in eyeglasses, streams of censors on their way to work, bloody corpses radiating out of Moscow) and the gentle Bonhoeffer. Almost miraculously I had crossed that invisible line beyond which people turn into actual readers, when they start to hear the voice of the writer as clearly as in a conversation. "Language," Tretsky had written, "is essentially a coercive act, and in the case of Eastern Europe it must be used as a tool to garden collective hopes and aspirations." As I read, with Solveig napping at the other end of the couch, I felt a thick dread forming. Tretsky, with his suggestions of annexations and, worse, of *solutions,* seemed to be reaching right off the page, his long, thin hand grasping me by the shirt. And I could almost hear the wild mazurka, as Stasselova had described it, fading, the cabarets closing down, the music turning into a chant, the boot heels falling, the language fortifying itself, becoming a stronghold—a fixed, unchanging system, as the paper said, a moral framework.

ALMOST IMMEDIATELY I WAS on my way to Stasselova's office, but not before my mother called. The golden brochures had gone out in the mail. "Sweetie!" she said. "What's this? Keynote speaker? Your father and I are beside ourselves. Good night!" She always exclaimed "Good night!" at times of great happiness. I could not dissuade her from coming, and as I fled the dorm, into the rare, hybrid air of early April, I was wishing for those bad, indifferent parents who had no real interest in their children's lives. The earth under my feet as I went to him was very sticky, almost lugubrious, like the earth one sometimes encounters in dreams. Stasselova was there, as always. He seemed pleased to see me.

I sat down and said, "You know, I was thinking that maybe somebody else could take my place at the symposium. As I reread my paper, I realized it isn't really what I meant to say at all."

"Oh," he said. "Of course you can deliver it. I would not abandon you at a moment like this."

"Really, I wouldn't take it as abandonment."

"I would not leave you in the lurch," he said. "I promise."

I felt myself being carried, mysteriously, into the doomed symposium, despite my resolve on the way over to back out at all costs. How could I win an argument against somebody with an early training in propaganda? I had to resort finally to the truth, that rinky-dink little boat in the great sea of persuasion. "See, I didn't really write the paper myself."

"Well, every thinker builds an idea on the backs of those before him—or her, in your case." He smiled at this. His teeth were very square, and humble, with small gaps between them. I could see that Stasselova was no longer after a confession. I was more valuable if I contained these ideas. Probably he'd been subconsciously looking for me ever since he'd lain on the muddy banks of the Vistula, Warsaw flaming across the waters. He could see within me all his failed ideals, the ugliness of his former beliefs contained in a benign vessel—a girl!—high on a religious hill in the Midwest. He had found somebody he might oppose and in this way absolve himself. He smiled. I could feel myself as indispensable in the organization of his psyche. Behind his head, in the sunset, the sun wasn't falling, only receding farther and farther.

THE DAYS BEFORE THE symposium unfurled like the days before a wedding one dreads, both endless and accelerated, the sky filled with springtime events—ravishing sun, great winds, and eccentric green storms that focused everyone's attention skyward. And then the weekend of the symposium was upon us, the Saturday of my speech rising in the east. I awoke early and went to practice my paper on the red steps of Humanities, in whose auditorium my talk was to take place. Solveig was still sleeping, hung over from the night before. I'd been with her for the first part of it, had watched her pursue a man she'd discovered—a graduate student, actually, in town for the symposium. I had thought him a bit of a bore, but I trusted Solveig's judgment. She approached men with stealth and insight, her vision driving into those truer, more isolated stretches of personality. I had practiced the paper countless times, and revised it, attempting to excise the most offensive lines without gutting the paper entirely and thus disappointing Stasselova. That morning I was still debating over the line "If we could agree on a common language, a single human tongue, perhaps then a single flag might fly over the excellent earth, one nation of like and companion souls." Reading it now, I had a faint memory of my earlier enthusiasm for this paper, its surface promise, its murderous innocence. Remembering this, I looked out over the excellent earth, at the town below the hill. And there, as always, was a tiny Gothic graveyard looking peaceful, everything still and settled finally under the gnarled, knotty, nearly human arms of apple trees. There were no apples yet, of course: they were making their way down the bough, still liquid, or whatever they are before birth. At the sight of graves I couldn't help thinking of Tretsky, my ghostwriter, in his dark suit under the earth, delightedly preparing, thanks to me, for his one last gasp.

By noon the auditorium had filled with a crowd of about two hundred, mostly graduate students and professors from around the Midwest, along with Hans and Solveig, who sat together, and, two rows behind them, my long-suffering parents, flushed with pride. I sat alone on a slight stage at the front of the room, staring out at the auditorium, which was named Luther. It had wooden walls and was extremely tall; it seemed humble and a little awkward, in that way the tall can seem. The windows stretched its full height, so that one could see the swell of earth on which Humanities was built, and then, above, all manner of weather, which this afternoon was running to rain. In front of these windows stood the reformed genius of martial law himself, the master of ceremonies, Stasselova. Behind him were maple trees, with small green leaves waving. He had always insisted in class that language as it rises in the mind looks like a tree branching, from finity to infinity. Let every voice cry out! He had once said this, kind of absently, and water had come to his eyes—not exactly tears, just a rising of the body's water into the line of sight.

After he introduced me, I stood in front of the crowd, my larynx rising quite against my will, and delivered my paper. I tried to speak each word as a discrete item, in order to persuade the audience not to synthesize the sentences into meaning. But when I lifted my head to look out at my listeners, I could see they were doing just that. When I got to the part where I said the individual did not exist— citizens were "merely shafts of light lost, redemptively, in the greater light of the state"—I saw Hans bow his head and rake his otherworldly hand through his hair.

"And if force is required to forge a singular and mutual grammar, then it is our sacred duty to hasten the birth pangs." Even from this distance I could hear Stasselova's breathing, and the sound of blood running through him like a quiet but rushing stream.

And then my parents. As the speech wore on—"harmony," "force," "flowering," "blood"—I could see that the very elegant parental machinery they had designed over the years, which sought always to translate my deeds into something lovely, light-bearing, full of promise, was spinning a little on its wheels. Only Solveig, that apparatchik of friendship, maintained her confidence in me. Even when she was hung over, her posture suggested a perfect alignment between heaven and earth. She kept nodding, encouraging me.

I waited the entire speech for Stasselova to leap forward and confront me, to reassert his innocence in opposition to me, but he did not, even when I reached the end. He stood and watched as everybody clapped in bewilderment, and a flushed floral insignia rose on his cheeks. I had come to love his wide, excited face, the old circus man. He smiled at me. He was my teacher, and he had wrapped himself, his elaborate historical self, into this package, and stood in front of the high windows, to teach me my little lesson, which turned out to be not about Poland or fascism or war, borderlines or passion or loyalty, but just about the sentence: the importance of, the sweetness of. And I did long for it, to say one true sentence of my own, to leap into the subject, that sturdy vessel traveling upstream through the axonal predicate into what is possible; into the object, which is all possibility; into what little we know of the future, of eternity—the light of which, incidentally, was streaming in on us just then through the high windows. Above Stasselova's head the storm clouds were dispersing, as if frightened by some impending goodwill, and I could see that the birds were out again, forming into that familiar pointy hieroglyph, as they're told to do from deep within.

Slatland

▼ ▼ ▼

I went to Professor Pine for help twice in my life, once as a child and once as an adult. The first time, I was eleven and had fallen into an inexplicable depression. This happened in the spring of 1967, seemingly overnight, and for no reason. Any happiness in me just flew away, like birds up and out of a tree.

Until then I had been a normal, healthy child. My parents had never damaged me in any way. They had given me a dusty, simple childhood on the flatlands of Saskatchewan. I had two best friends — large, unselfish girls who were already gearing up for adolescence, sometimes laughing until they collapsed. I had a dog named Chest, who late at night brought me half-alive things in his teeth—bats with human faces, fluttering birds, speckled, choking mice.

My parents couldn't help noticing my sadness. They looked at me as if they were afraid of me. Sometimes at the dinner table the silence would be so deep that I felt compelled to reassure them. But when I tried to say that I was all right, my voice would crack and I would feel my face distorting, caving in. I would close my eyes then, and cry.

One night my parents came into my bedroom and sat down on my bed. "Honey," my father said, "your mother and I have been thinking about you a lot lately. We were thinking that maybe you would consider talking to somebody—you know, a therapist—about what is the matter." My father was an earnest, cheerful man, a geologist with a brush cut and a big heart. I couldn't imagine that a therapist would solve my problems, but my father looked hopeful, his large hand tracing a ruffle around my bedspread.

Three days later we were standing outside an office on the fourth floor of the Humanities Building. My appointment was not with a true therapist but rather with a professor of child psychology at the university where my father taught.

We knocked, and a voice called from behind the door in a bit of a singsong, "Come in you, come in you." Of course he was expecting us, but this still seemed odd, as if he knew us very well or as if my father and I were both little children—or elves. The man sitting behind the desk when we entered was wearing a denim shirt, his blond hair slicked back like a rodent's. He looked surprised—a look that turned out to be permanent. He didn't stand up, just waved at us. From a cage in the corner three birds squawked. My father approached the desk and stuck out his hand. "Peter Bergen," my father said.

"Professor Roland Boland Pine," the man said, and then looked at me. "Hello, girlie."

Despite this, my father left me alone with him. Perhaps he just thought, as I did, that Professor Pine talked like this, in occasional baby words, because he wanted children to respond as if to other children. I sat in a black leather chair. The professor and I just stared at each other for a while. I didn't know what to say, and he wasn't speaking either. It was easy to stare at him. As if I were staring at an animal, I felt no embarrassment.

"Well," he said at last, "your name is Margit?"

I nodded.

"How are you today, Margit?"

"I'm okay."

"Do you feel okay?"

"Yes. I feel okay."

"Do you go to school, Margit?"

"Yes."

"Do you like your teacher?"

"Not really."

"Do you hate him?"

"It's a her."

"Do you hate her?"

"No."

"Why are you here, Margit?"

"I don't know."

"Is everything okay at home?"

"Yes."

"Do you love your father?"

"Yes."

"Do you love your mother?" A long tic broke on his face, from the outer corner of his left eye all the way down to his neck.

"Yes."

"Is she a lumpy mother?"

"Pardon me?"

"Pardon me, Margit. I meant does your mother love you?"

"Yes."

"Does she love your father?"

I paused. "Yes."

"And does he love her?"

"I guess so."

"Margit, what is the matter?"

"Nothing. I just don't see why we're talking about my parents so much."

"Why don't they love each other?"

"They do—I said they do."

"Why can't you talk about this?"

"Because there's nothing to talk about."

"You can tell me the truth. Do they hurt each other? Lots of girls' parents hurt each other."

"No, they don't."

"Is one of them having an affair, maybe?"

I didn't say anything. "Maybe?" he repeated.

"Maybe," I said.

"Which one, Margit? Which one of the babyfaces?"

I stared at him. Another tic passed over his face. "Pardon me, Margit. I meant which one of your parents is having the affair?"

"My dad. But I don't think he's actually having it. I just heard him tell my mom a few months ago that he was considering it."

"And do you think he is?"

"I don't know. A few weeks ago I picked up the phone and a woman was talking to my dad. She told him that she had to have her breasts removed and asked if that would make a difference."

"How difficult for you. How sad for the girlie-whirl." Another tic, like a fault line shifting. "Margit, may I tell you something from my own childhood?"

This worried me, but I said yes.

"When I was young, I loved my mother. She was a real lumper. Then one day, kerpow, she was dead." He held his forefinger to his head as if it were the barrel of a gun and stared at me for a few seconds without speaking. "It wasn't actually her, you see, but a woman of about her age who happened to be walking toward me on the sidewalk. A man came running and shot her. I was so devastated that I fell right on top of her. I didn't care if he shot me, too. I was only ten at the time, and my mother's death could have scarred me for life. But it didn't. And do you know how I got from that moment to this one—how I got from there to here, to sitting behind this desk now, talking to you?"

I shook my head. "How?"

"I rose above the situation. Literally I did. I felt my mind lift out of my body, and I stared down at myself leaning over the bleeding woman. I said to myself, very calmly, there is little Roland from New Orleans, the little erky-terk, realizing that someday his mother will die."

He was looking at me so intently, and his birds were flapping in their cage with such fervor, that I felt I had to say something. "Wow," I said.

"I suggest you try it, Margit. For every situation there is a proper distance. Growing up is just a matter of gaining perspective. Sometimes you just need to jump up for a moment, a foot above the earth. And sometimes you need to jump very far. It is as if there are thin slats, footholds, from here to the sun, Margit, for the baby faces to step on. Do you understand?"

"Yes," I said.

"Slatland, flatland, mapland."

"Pardon me?"

"Pardon me, Margit. I know so many languages that sometimes I say words out of place."

At the end of the session I asked him when I should return. He told me that another visit wouldn't be necessary, that usually his therapy worked the first time.

I didn't in fact understand what he had said to me, but his theory seemed to help anyway, as if it were a medication that worked whether you understood it or not. That very evening I was having dinner with my parents. It started as the usual dinner—me staring at my plate, my parents staring at me as if I were about to break in two. But about halfway through the meal I started feeling light-headed. Nothing frightening happened, but I did manage to lift slightly out of myself. I looked down at our tiny family. I saw my father from above, the deep map of his face. I understood in an instant that of course he was having an affair, and that he was torn between my mother and this other, distant woman. I saw my beautiful mother from above, and I could see how she must hate this other woman, yet sympathize as well, because this other woman was very ill. I understood how complicated it was to be an adult, and how haunting, and how lovely. I longed to be back in my body then, to be breathing and eating, straining toward maturity. And when I returned, one split second later, I hugged my parents, one after the other, with a spontaneity that a depressed person could never muster.

In the twenty years that passed between my first visit to Professor Pine and my second, from 1967 to 1987, I remained in the same city. I graduated from Massey and then from LeBoldus High and then from the University of Saskatchewan, with a degree in biology. As an adult, I worked as a soil consultant, traveling around the province to small satellite towns in a flatbed truck that I could sleep in, if necessary, on warm nights.

Bouts of the depression did return, but they never overwhelmed me. Perhaps my life was not the most rigorous testing ground for Professor Pine's technique, because my life was relatively free of tragedy. Most of my depression erupted out of nowhere. I'd be in the fields in the midst of a bright day, and a dreariness would mysteriously descend. I'd sink into it for a few minutes, but the lift would always come. I would take a step up, or two or three, and recognize how good life in fact was. From above, my job appeared to me excellent and strange. There I was, under a blazing sun, kneeling in a yellow expanse, weighing samples of earth. And later, with instruments as tiny and beautiful as jewelry, testing the dirt for traces of nitrogen and phosphorus, the gleam of potash.

One night, in the middle of the year 1985, I made the mistake of describing this technique to my fiancé, Rezvan Balescu, the Romanian liar. We had known each other for only two months at this point, but we were already engaged. We were standing on a small balcony outside our apartment. He was smoking, wearing pajamas under a down-filled jacket, and he was in the midst of one of his tirades on North America, which he loved and hated. "This place is so strange to me, so childish. You have so many problems that are not real, and you are so careful and serious about them. People discuss their feelings as if they were great works of art or literature that need to be analyzed and examined and passed on and on. In my country people love or they hate. They know that a human being is mysterious, and they live with that. The problems they have are real problems. If you do not eat, that's a problem. If you have no leg, that's a problem. If you are unhappy, that is not a problem to talk about."

"I think it is," I said.

"Exactly. That is because you are an American. For you, big things are small, and small things are big." Rezvan was always making these large declarations about North Americans in a loud voice from our balcony.

"I bet you one million in money," Rezvan said as he blew out smoke, "that the number of hours Americans spend per week in these—what do you call them?—therapy offices is exactly the same number of hours Romanians spend in line for bread. And for what? Nothing. To make their problems bigger. They talk about them all day so at night they are even bigger."

"I don't agree. The reason why people talk about their

problems is to get over them, get rid of them. I went to a therapist once and he was very helpful."

"You?" He lifted an eyebrow, took a drag.

"Yes, when I was eleven."

"Eleven? What could be the problem at eleven?"

"I was just sad. My parents were getting divorced, and I guess I could tell that my dad was about to leave."

"But isn't that the correct emotion — sadness — when a father leaves? Can a therapist do anything to bring your father home?"

"No, but he gave me a way to deal with it."

"And what is that way? I would like to know."

"Well, just a way to separate from the situation."

"How do you separate from your own life?"

"Well, you rise above it. You gain some objectivity and perspective."

"But is this proper? If you have a real problem, should you rise above it? When a father leaves a child, the child feels sad. This seems right to me. This rising above, that is the problem. In fact, that is the problem of America. I cannot tell my family back home that if they are hungry or cold, they should just rise above it. I cannot say, 'Don't worry, go to the movies, go shop, here is ten dollars in money, go buy some candy. Rise above your situation.' "

"That's not what I mean. I mean you literally rise above it. Your mind hovers over your body, and you understand the situation from a higher perspective." I knew that if he pushed me far enough, this would end up sounding insane.

"So this is what your man, your eleven-year-old therapist, teaches you: to separate your mind from your body, to become unhinged. This does not teach you to solve the problem; this teaches you to be a crazy person."

But already I was drifting up until I was watching us from the level of the roof. There she is, I thought, Margit Bergen, twenty-nine years old, in love with Rezvan of Romania, a defector who escaped political hardship to arrive in a refugee camp in Austria and a year later in Regina, Saskatchewan, where he now stands on a balcony in the moonlight, hassling her about America, as if she contained all of it inside her.

I HAD MET REZVAN in my father's lab at the university. Rezvan was a geologist, like my father. Technically, for grant reasons, he was a graduate student, but my father considered him a peer, because Rezvan had already worked for years as a geologist for the Romanian government.

Originally he had been a supporter of Ceauşescu. In fact, his father, Andrei, had been a friend of Ceauşescu's right up until the time Andrei died, in 1985. Rezvan, by his own account, stood by his father's deathbed as he died and held his father's hand, but both father and son refused to speak, because Rezvan had by then ceased to be loyal to Ceauşescu.

In the two years that Rezvan and I lived together, I would often rise from sleep to find him hunched over his desk, the arm of his lamp reaching over him. He wrote long letters into the night, some in English and some in Romanian. The English ones, he said, were to various government officials, asking for help in getting his family over to Canada. The ones in Romanian were to his family, an assortment of aunts and uncles and cousins. He wrote quickly, as in a fever, and if I crept up on him and touched his back, he would jump and turn over his letters immediately before looking up at me in astonishment. At the time, I thought this was simply an old habit of fear, left over from living for so long in a police state.

Sometimes he said he could not forgive his country for keeping his family captive. He told what he called jokes—dark, labyrinthine stories that always ended with some cartoonish, undignified death for Ceauşescu: his head in a toilet, his body flattened by a steamroller. Other times he spoke about his country with such longing—the wet mist of Transylvania, the dark tunnels beneath the streets of his town, the bookstores lined with propaganda that opened into small, dusty rooms in back filled with real books.

In this same way Rezvan loved and hated America. He would rant about it from the balcony, but then we would return to our bed and sit side by side, our backs to the wall, and watch the local and then the national news, where almost every night somebody would criticize the prime minister, Brian Mulroney. Rezvan could never get over this: men appearing on television to insult their leader night after night and never getting pulled off the air. Sometimes we would turn to the news from the United States, which we received through a cable channel from Detroit. This was a real treat for Rezvan during the period of Reagan-bashing. "I love that man," he said to me one night.

"Reagan? You don't like Reagan."

"I know, but look at him now." They were showing a clip of Reagan waving. His face did look kind. His eyes were veering off, looking skyward. He looked like some-body's benevolent, faintly crazy grandfather.

"All day long people insult him and he doesn't kill any of them."

Rezvan sometimes skipped work and came with me to the fields. He'd ride in the back of the truck, standing up, so that his head was above the cab, the wind pouring over him. He wanted to know all the details of my job. He became better than I was at some things. He could spot poor field drainage from far away. He loved to point out the signs of it—the mint, the rushes, the wiregrass, the willows.

For lunch we stopped in the towns along the way at small, fragrant home-style diners. Almost all of them were run by Ukrainian women. Each one adored Rezvan. He would kiss their hands and speak in his strange accent—part British, part Romanian—and they would serve him free platefuls of food, one after another, hovering over him as if he were a long-lost son from the old country.

One afternoon, while we were driving back to the city from a little town called Yellow Grass, I fell asleep at the wheel. I woke up after the crash to see Rezvan crumpled against the passenger door. I felt myself rising then, far above the car, far above even the tree line. From there I watched myself crawl out of the wreck and drag Rezvan out onto the grassy shoulder. And then, instead of watching my own body run down the long charcoal highway, I stayed above Rezvan. I watched the trees bow in the wind toward his body, listening for his heartbeat.

Later that night, when I entered his hospital room for the first time, I expected him to refuse to speak to me. Rezvan smiled, though. "In my country," he said, "you could work for Ceaușescu. He has been trying to do this to me for years." I started apologizing then, over and over. Rezvan just motioned me toward the bed and then put his arms around me. "It's okay, it's okay," he said. "Don't cry. This is America. This is what is supposed to happen. I will sue you, and your insurance will give us money, and we will go on a trip. To California, a vacation. I am so happy."

I wiped my eyes and looked at him. His head was cocked to the side. A thin white bandage was wrapped around his forehead, and blood was still matted in the black curls of his hair. One side of his face was torn apart. His leg was suspended in a sling. Still, he looked at me incredulously, wondering how I could be crying when this was such a stroke of luck.

For the next few months he had a cane, which he loved. He liked to point at things with it. The scars settled into faint but permanent tracks down the left side of his face. He liked that, too. We saw the movie *Scarface* over and over again. When he discarded the cane, he still walked with a slight limp, which gave his gait an easy rocking motion that seemed strangely to suit him. He never once blamed me; I don't think it ever crossed his mind.

REZVAN AND I STAYED engaged for two years. He seemed to think of engagement as an alternative to marriage rather than as a lead-up to it. I didn't mind, actually. I just wanted to be with him. Life with Rezvan had a sort of gloss to it always. He passed quickly from emotion to emotion, from sadness to gratitude to arrogance, but he never fell into depression, ever.

Perhaps because I was so happy with Rezvan, I did not notice what may have been obvious signs. But, oddly enough, the signs indicating that a man is in love with another woman are often similar to the signs of an immigrant in a new country, his heart torn in two. He wrote long letters home; he hesitated to talk about the future; during lonely nights he seemed to be murmuring as he fell asleep, but not to me.

Nearly a year passed before I even noticed anything,

or admitted to myself that I noticed anything. Then one day Rezvan received a phone call at four in the morning. I didn't understand a word of it, since it was in Romanian, but in my half sleep I could hear him mutter the word *rila* again and again, sometimes insistently. And when he hung up, after about an hour and a half, he just sat there in the living room like a paralyzed man, the light slowly rising across his body. I asked him, "Rezvan, what does *rila* mean?" He told me that it meant "well lit," as in a room.

Two days later, as I walked up our driveway in my housecoat, the mail in my hand, I glanced through the letters and noticed a thick letter from Rilia Balescu. Rila was Rilia, a person, a relative. When I walked in the door, Rezvan was standing in his striped pajamas drinking coffee, smoking, scratching his head. As I handed him the letter, I tried to read his face, but saw nothing. So I said, "Who is Rilia?"

"She is my sister, my baby sister. Gavrilia."

Does an extra beat pass before one tells a lie? This is what I had always believed, but Rezvan answered immediately. Perhaps he had been waiting for the question.

"I didn't know you had a sister."

"I don't like to talk about her. We disowned each other long ago. She follows Ceauşescu still; she has pictures of him and his son on her wall as if they were rock stars. I am trying to bring her over, but she is stubborn. She would rather go to the Black Sea and vacation with her boys than come here and live with me."

"So why have you never told me about her?"

"Because it is not wise to speak aloud the one thing you want more than anything. You know that."

"No, I don't know that."

"It's true. Romanians have a word for it: *ghinion.* It means don't speak aloud what you want most. Otherwise it will not happen. You must have a word for this in English?"

"Jinx."

"Okay. I did not tell you about my sister because of jinx."

"Why did you tell me her name meant 'well lit'?"

"Pardon?"

"The other day I asked you, and you said that 'Rilia' was the word for 'well lit.'"

"No, no. *Rila* is the word for 'well lit.' Rilia is my sister." He smiled and kissed my face. "We will have to work on your accent."

Over the next month we settled into a routine. When Rezvan finished writing his letters in the night, he padded down the driveway, set the letters in the mailbox, and lifted the tiny, stiff red flag so that our mailman would stop in the morning. And then, after Rezvan was asleep, I would rise out of bed and go to the mailbox myself, pick out the ones to Rilia, and slip them into the pocket of my housecoat. I did the same thing with the letters she sent him. I collected those in the morning.

At first it didn't feel like a strategy. I was desperate to know if Rilia really was his sister or his wife—as if her handwriting would tell me. Rezvan left for work an hour before I did, and I opened the letters then. I sat on our bed, laying the pages in front of me, cross-referencing. Some of her passages were blacked out by censors. I found many names, but mostly two, Gheorghe and Florian, again and again. Gheorghe and Florian, Gheorghe and Florian, Gheorghe and Florian. I began to realize, very slowly, that these were probably their children.

On one of these mornings my mother showed up at my door to drop off a skirt she had sewed for me. "Good," she said, bustling in, "you're home. I wanted to drop this off." Already, as she said this, she was rapidly moving through the rooms of our apartment. My mother liked to do this, to catch me off guard and check all my rooms immediately for anything I might hide if given the time. "What is this?" she said, reaching the bedroom, where all the pages were strewn across the bed.

"Oh, that's just some stuff I'm reading for Rezvan. Proofreading."

She picked up a sheet. "Oh, so now you proofread in Romanian?"

I smiled weakly. She didn't pry, but for once I wished she would. What I wanted to do was tell her that this was my life spread across the bed, thin as paper, written in a language I could not understand, dotted with four names—

Rezvan, Gavrilia, Gheorghe, Florian—but never my own. I wanted to ask her how she felt when my father was having an affair. And I wanted to ask what happened to the other woman. My father never married her, even after he and my mother split. Where had she drifted off to? Did she ever lose her breasts? Did she get well again? Was she happy somewhere now?

I didn't tell my mother anything, but when she left that day, she gestured toward the bedroom. "You know that you can find people at the university who will translate that for you."

I nodded and stared at my feet.

"Maybe you don't really need them translated? Maybe you already know what they say?" She ducked her face under, so that she could look at my face. "It'll be okay," she said, "either way."

I stockpiled the letters for two months. I didn't intend to be malicious; I was just sitting on them until I could figure out what to do. Every night as I drove home from the fields, I thought, I will tell Rezvan tonight; I will say I know everything and I am leaving. But when dinner came, I could hardly speak. It was as if I were eleven all over again.

Even Rezvan was getting depressed. He said that his letters were turning out to be all in vain. Perhaps, he said, he would quit writing them altogether. One night he said, "Nothing gets through those bastards. Perhaps I will never see Rilia again." Then he limped to the sink, rocking back and forth, and filled his glass with water. He turned to me and said, "Why would they want to keep us apart, anyway?" His head was tilted to the side, and he looked like a child. He stared at me as if he really expected me to answer.

"I don't know," I said. "I don't know about that stuff."

But of course I did. At the other end, across the ocean, men in uniforms were collecting letters and censoring them, blacking out whatever threatened them, and at this end I in my housecoat was doing the same thing.

I tried to rise above the situation, but that strategy didn't work at all. I was increasingly distressed at what I saw. I'd fly up and look down. There she is, I'd say, Margit Bergen of Saskatchewan. Who would have thought she'd grow up so crooked, crouched on her bed, obstructing love, hoarding it, tearing it apart with her own hands.

Until this point in my life I had always thought of myself as an open-minded person, able to step into another's shoes. But I could not picture this Rilia. Her face, and the faces of her children, were blank for me. I hoped that this inability, or unwillingness, to imagine another's face was not hatred, but I was deeply ashamed that it might be.

Finally, one windy night in November, as I cut into a roast, I said, "Rezvan, is Rilia your wife?"

"What do you know of Rilia? Has she called? Has she sent a letter?"

"No, not at all. I was just wondering."

"Tell me what you know."

"I don't know anything. I was just asking."

"Have you spoken to her on the phone?"

"No, I have not." I enunciated this very clearly. "Is she your wife, Rezvan?"

"I am not a liar," he said. "I will marry you to prove this. We will go to British Columbia and get married in the trees. Whenever you want. Tomorrow, if you like."

THE NEXT MORNING I put the letters in a bag and drove straight to the administrative offices at the university. A woman disappeared and reappeared with a list of professors who could translate Romanian for me. I had my choice of four. I glanced down the list and there, at number three, was Professor Roland Pine.

I found him in the same office. He had aged well, his hair now ash instead of blond, a few extra lines across his face. When he stood up to greet me, I say that I had grown to be about half a foot taller than he was. His tic was still there, flashing across his face every fifteen seconds or so. As I shook his hand, I marveled that it had continued like this since the last time I'd seen him, keeping time as faithfully as a clock.

"My name is Margit Bergen. I came to you once as a child."

"Hello, Margit. It's nice to see you again. Was I helpful?"

"Yes, very. I've always been grateful."

"What was the problem in those days?"

"Just childhood depression, I guess. My parents were splitting up."

He squinted at me, and turned his face slightly to the side. "Oh, yes," he said. "That's right. Of course. Little Margit. You were such a girlie-whirl. So sad. What did you become?"

"You mean in my life?"

"In your life. What did you become?"

"A soil consultant."

"What a good job for you." He gestured toward the black leather chair. His birds fought in their high cages, their wings tearing at each other. "Mortalhead. You be nice to Eagerheart." He turned to me. "The kids love funny names, you know. Mortalhead, Eagerheart, Quickeye."

I smiled and sat down in the chair, pulling a stack of letters from my bag. "Professor Pine," I said.

"Call me Roland," he said. He leaned back. His face cracked in a tic. "Roland Boland. Just think: little Roland and little Margit, the professor and the soil consultant, back again, sitting in a warm office surrounded by bird-people." He rolled his eyes and grinned, almost girlishly.

I didn't know what to say. "Yes, it's nice," I eventually said. "Actually, Roland, I was wondering if you could help me out with a problem I have."

"I thought I solved all your problems." He looked disappointed.

"You did. I mean, for twenty years you did."

"What could be the problem now?"

"I need you to translate these letters for me, from Romanian."

"Romanian?" He took the stack of letters from me, and began to leaf through them. "Is your name Rezvan?" he said.

"He's a friend of mine."

"Then you should not read his letters." He smiled.

"Professor Pine, I really need you to do this for me."

"Who is Rilia?"

"I don't know. Look, you don't even need to read them to me. Just read them to yourself and tell me if the people writing them are married."

"Why do you want to know?"

"That doesn't matter. I just do."

"Why?"

I didn't say anything.

"Are you being a dirty-girlie?" He smiled—and then a tic, as forked as lightning.

I sighed and looked over at his birds, who were cawing loudly. One was green with black wings, and it was flapping furiously, staring at the letters fluttering in Professor Pine's hand.

"Fine, Professor Pine. If you don't want to read them, I'll take them to somebody else." I reached for the letters.

He pulled them back, toward his chest. "Okay, okay, girlie," he said. "You are so stubborn, Margit."

He read softly, in a lilting voice, as if he were reading me a bedtime story. "Rilia says, 'Remember how tiny Florian was at his birth? Now he is forty-five kilos, the same as his brother.' Rilia says, 'Remember the Black Sea, it is as blue as the first time we went to it.' Rilia says that Rezvan must be lying when he says there is so much food that sometimes he tosses rotten fruit from the window."

I interrupted. "Do you think they are married?"

"Well, they are both Balescus."

"They could be brother and sister?"

He frowned, and leafed through the letters again. "But here she calls him darling. Darling, barling, starling."

He looked up then. "Oh, no," he said, "don't cry. Please don't cry." He jumped up, came around the side of the desk, and crouched beside my chair. He looked up at me. His face was close, and the next tic was like slow motion. I saw the path that it followed, curving and winding like a river down his face.

He sat back on the edge of his desk. "It's going to be okay," he said. "We just have to figure out what the girlie wants. If you want Rezvan, the liar face, you can have him. Is that what you want?"

"No, I don't think so. I mean, I do, but I can't. He has kids and everything."

"Then it sounds like you've made up your mind already."

"Not really," I said.

"Margit, you need some perspective."

"Perspective?"

"You know"—he rolled his eyes upward—"Slatland."

Slatland—I remembered that that was what he'd called it, the drifting up and looking down.

"I've tried Slatland. It didn't work," I said.

"Slatland always works. Just close your eyes, all right, girlie?"

I started to stand up. "Thanks for your help, Professor Pine. I really have to go now." But then I felt it, the lift, and my mind started rising, until the caws of Mortalhead and Eagerheart and Quickeye were far below me. I could see the yellow fields surrounding my town, and then even those went out of focus. I hurtled faster and faster until I finally stopped, what seemed like minutes later.

So this is Slatland, I thought. I looked down, and to my left I saw North America, large and jagged, flanked by oceans. Its face was beautiful—craggy, broken, lined with rivers. I found my part of the continent, a flat gold rectangle in the upper middle. I saw what my daily life looked like from this distance: my truck beetling through the prairies, dust rising off its wheels the way desire must rise, thousands of fragments of stone lifting off the earth. And when the truck stopped and I stepped out into the bright, empty fields, my loneliness looked extreme. I could almost see it, my longing and desire for Rezvan rising out of me the way a tree rises out of its trunk. I perceived, in an instant, exactly what I should do to keep him. I saw how simple it all would be, just to keep collecting the letters every morning, one by one, in order that what was between Rezvan and his wife would die slowly and easily and naturally, and what was between him and me would grow in exactly the same proportion.

If I had been able to climb down then, to drop out of Slatland at that moment, everything would have remained simple, and probably Rezvan and I would still be together. But Slatland seemed to have a will of its own. It would not let me go until I looked down to my right. If I was willing to see the simplicity, the purity, of my own desire, then I also had to see the entire landscape—the way desire rises from every corner and intersects, creates a wilderness over the earth.

I stood on Slatland a long time before I looked down to my right. There is was, Eastern Europe, floating above the Mediterranean. I traced with my finger the outline of Romania. I squinted, down through the mist and mountains, down through the thick moss of trees, until I found her. She stood in a long line of people, her forty-five-kilo children hanging on her skirts. She bent to them and broke for them some bread as hard as stone. I hovered a few feet above her and watched. Even so, I might still have been able to return to my own life, my own province, unchanged if she hadn't turned her face upward right then, as if she had felt some rain, and looked directly at me.

This all happened very fast, in a blink of my eyes. When I opened them, Professor Pine was sitting on his desk, watching me. "You're a real erky-terk," he said, with a tic so extreme that it looked like it might swallow his face. He walked me to the door and handed me the letters, which later that night I would give to Rezvan. We would be standing on the balcony in the semidarkness of the moon, and I would be surprised at how easily they passed through my hands, as easily as water.

The birds shrieked. "Birdmen!" Professor Pine said. "Sometimes I feel like saluting them," he said to me. He shook my hand. "Good luck, girlie-whirl." Then he went up on his tiptoes and kissed me good-bye.

MIN

▼ ▼ ▼

I sat on a metal folding chair, facing the five members of the Student-Faculty Relations Committee—one dean, two professors, and two students. Sunshine poured in. Carved in the wall above their heads were the words *"Animus non integritatem sed facinus cupit,"* meaning "The heart wills not purity but adventure."

Despite the sun, it was snowing outside—big delicate flakes. This was early February 1989, not a good year for romance. At least not in American universities.

"Would you describe your relationship with Professor Harrison as *intimate,* then?" This was the dean, a large, gentle man.

"Perhaps intimate, yes," I said. Harrison, with whom I

spent every Tuesday and Thursday in a seminar on Rilke, was an elegant, vaguely licentious man, whom I thought exuded longing for all things, not merely his female students. Truthfully, I was embarrassed to be here. I had been subpoenaed along with eleven other women, most of whom had complex stories to tell about Harrison. But he had made only a couple of standard passes at me. And I might have fallen for them had I not known he made passes regularly, almost randomly. His mistake with me, I admit, was less ethical than strategic.

"Would you describe Professor Harrison's attention as inappropriate?" asked Catherine Stole, a tall, cool woman. The previous semester I had attended her class on feminist literary theory.

"Somewhat inappropriate, yes," I said, "but not offensive."

"Not offensive?" She raised her eyebrows and looked at me disapprovingly, as if she were failing me retroactively. I stared back, maintaining silently that there was a place, even if just a thin window, where inappropriate and offensive did not intersect.

"I would have been flattered," said Min Leung, one of the students on the committee. He was an incredibly handsome man with a wide, bronze face, and he spoke happily, as if we were all just chatting. Everybody looked at him. He smiled and shrugged.

I saw Min again a week later, in the grocery store, tossing a tomato in the air. "One of the harassment girls," he said. "Hello, I forget your name."

"Sarah Johnson," I said. "And you are Min Leung."

"Yes," he said. We shook hands.

"It must have been quite dull to sit through all that," I said.

"Oh no," he said. "It was fascinating."

"Fascinating?"

"Where I am from, to be desired is a great honor. In fact, the one who is desired feels immense gratitude, particularly if the one who desires is in a position of authority. The one who is desired showers the one who desires with gifts, sometimes for many years. Out of gratitude."

I was eating green grapes from a plastic bag. I smiled as I tried to imagine all of us carrying gifts to Harrison's home, year after year.

Nothing official happened to Harrison, but as winter passed into spring, I did notice him attempt to gaze across our classroom with a lesser trace of desire in his pale blue eyes. Meanwhile, outside the windows, our rolling religious campus gathered heat and moisture until it suddenly grew everywhere a velvety green grass. In the midst of the warm, humid spring Min and I became excellent and permanent friends.

Min was a rare man. His personality was composed of

both arrogance and a gentle gratitude. He wore the same thing every day: Levi's, a white button-down shirt, and a black leather jacket. He had a motorcycle, and most evenings after dinner we went for long rides, into the dusky, sloppy countryside of southern Montana. We usually ended up at the cliffs, about a half-hour ride from campus.

One of these nights, as we sat on a granite cliff, a sad line of cows moved in among the waters below us. The big bells around their necks rang. The sun was slung low in the distance. "I will miss this," Min said. He pulled a couple of beers out of his backpack and gave me one. "And you?" he said, smiling through the dark. "What will you do without me?"

"Could you stay the summer at least?"

He shook his head. "My father," he said.

I nodded. Min's father had found Min a job in his office that summer, and I knew, as well, that Min was worried about his father. A couple of months earlier, in mid-March, he had shown me an article in the *New York Times* that included a quotation from his father, Albert Leung. The quotation was brief and lyrical, and it carried the same sort of kindness and sadness that I would later discover in Albert himself: "We regret, as a colony, our inability to overcome compassion fatigue."

Min's father had been recommended by Margaret Thatcher to Hong Kong's Legislative Council in 1984. He worked in the council department that handled refugees arriving in Hong Kong. Most were Vietnamese, a group that had been arriving steadily since the fall of Saigon, in 1975. In the past couple of years, however, the number of refugees streaming in had risen sharply, causing a severe crisis.

A couple of times I had watched Min answer the phone when his father called. Min would shout a warm "*Ni hao!*" into the phone and then fall silent. He would end the conversation in a low, staccato Cantonese.

"Sarah," Min said suddenly. "Why don't you come with me?"

I shook my head. "I'd love to, but I'm broke. Next summer, maybe."

"Next summer I'll be married."

I blinked. "You're engaged?"

"Not yet. It will be arranged."

"An arranged marriage? No kidding? That's depressing, Min."

"Not necessarily."

"What if you don't like her?"

"Then I won't marry her. It only means that somebody will sift through the possibilities for me, with my best interests at heart."

"And whom do you trust to do this?"

"Officially the father decides; unofficially the mother. But since my mother is dead, the unofficial screening has fallen to my father. He's quite nervous about it."

"I guess. What a job."

Min sat down. "Sarah, listen, my father will pay for your flight."

"I'd feel funny taking your father's money."

"Then he'll give you a job. With me."

"I'm not really qualified to organize refugee relief."

"Well, who is?" he said, shrugging and grinning. "So it's settled, then?" He leaned forward to kiss my cheek. His face was beautiful, with one thick vein running down his forehead, around his left eye.

"Maybe," I said, and then we sat silent for a while, Min's foot drumming a little beat in the dirt. I said, "Min, I can't believe that."

"What?"

"That your marriage will be arranged. Don't you believe in desire?"

"Of course. My grandparents went the length of China with everything they owned on their backs on the basis of nothing but desire. But I can't imagine them looking to *create* desire in their relationship. Their lives were saturated with desire; they were looking to carefully, intelligently *ṣlake* it. You see?" he tipped back his head and took a long swallow of beer. Behind him the orange sun had lit the length of the horizon, like wildfire.

"Anyway," he said, "romance bores me." He raised his head regally, and waved his hand as if flicking something away. Then he smiled at me, paused a few moments, and said, "You will love my city."

OUR ROUTE WAS MISSOULA to L.A. and then west over the Pacific to Hong Kong. We went Northwest first class—huge, plush chairs, bowls of sherbet on china followed by tea every couple of hours. Liquor was free, so Min and I drank it liberally. Over the course of that night, including our long stopover in Seoul, we became tipsy and sober again three times as we drifted in and out of daylight.

I was sure we would tear off the tips of the buildings as we descended straight into the heart of Hong Kong. Landing was intensely exotic, like swiftly entering a jewel, a ruby.

Albert was there to meet us. As soon as Min saw his father, he grabbed my hand and we rushed through the crowd. When Albert and Min hugged each other, I noticed that Albert was hugging with only one arm. The other was slack at his side. He'd apparently had a stroke.

Min pulled back. "Dad," he said, "are you all right?"

"Oh, yes, only a small accident. It's healing rapidly." He continued to pat Min on the back as he turned to me. "And you must be Sarah. I'm always honored to meet a friend of my son's."

"Thank you," I said. "Thank you for inviting me."

Moments later I was in the soft leather backseat of

Albert's silver-blue Jaguar, passing under the electric can-
opy of Nathan Road, breathing in the scent of the city,
which was—in equal parts—diesel exhaust, rank mango
from the pyramids stacked on the sidewalks, and the keen
salty air that rose off the Pacific.

We passed through the tunnel to Hong Kong Island
and drove down a quiet street lined with inverted pines,
stopping at a dark-blue, turreted restaurant. Over dinner
I discovered that Albert, like Min, was a curious, gracious
man with a talent for asking personal questions that one
might want to answer. Albert and Min got along well. As
they talked, I studied their faces.

They looked alike, though racially they were obviously
not identical. Albert, I knew, was pure Chinese. His family
had once been refugees to Hong Kong from Manchouli,
a northern city in Manchuria province, close to both
Mongolia and the Soviet Union. Min's mother had been
from a tiny mountain town in the Himalayas, above Nepal.
I wondered how that would be, to be a father and to stare
across a table, through the crackling candlelight, and see
your own face, younger, broadened and transformed by
both time and race. How interesting it would be to see the
future that precisely.

Albert lived in Kowloon, which is on the mainland, so
we passed back and began our steady climb upward, out of
the lit city, into a dark, densely wooded area on the periphery

called Clear Water. The house was green and sprawling, overlooking a small back of the South China Sea.

All around us rose small, jagged mountains. In the dark they looked alive, like giant blackbirds, staring down at their one treasure—the little sapphire bay.

MIN AND I HAD a week before we began our jobs. We set out the first morning in Albert's Jaguar. Once downtown, we roamed on foot. The first street we stepped into was steep and lined with small stands selling slices of snake to eat and the bodies of fish that supposedly had been drawn from the ocean decades ago, in the 1950s. This was a delicacy, and if one ate it carefully, it would give a specific sort of knowledge, the fish-seller said, knowledge that all desire is one day satisfied. "Why?" Min asked.

"Why?" The man raised his eyebrows.

"Why will this fish give us this knowledge?"

"Because a fish's desire is be eaten, and this fish has waited all these years." He seemed to have made this up on the spot.

"Seems counterintuitive," Min said.

The man looked annoyed with us, so we moved on. I carried the fish. It did have a sort of sad, waiting look to it. I took a bite. The texture was webby, bristly. It had a layer of crystalline, almost invisible salt, and my throat tightened against it.

"Mmm," I said to Min. "It's working already. Have a bite."

Min took a bite, and made a gagging noise. We sucked on it for a while, until an incredible thirst overtook us both. I didn't want to throw it out uneaten, though, in case what the fish-seller had said was true. "Wrap it up," Min said. "Send it to your sad Mr. Harrison. He'll eat it." I smiled and eventually set it down in the gutter for a stray cat.

We passed into the next street, which was, suddenly, a thoroughfare lined with marble-and-glass skyscrapers. The rest of the week would pass exactly like this—each street a small, soft shock. Because I was from the prairies, a city built on hills struck me as voluptuous, revealing. Beyond a row of gray shanties I could see a beautiful pink mansion on a hill, and beyond that another hill with a dark Catholic crucifix rising from it, and beyond that the Hindu monks crawling up a slope, tilling a small plot of berries. And every day I would see, here and there, the long silver barracks of the refugee camps, shining and surrounded by barbed wire.

I read in the *Hong Kong Standard* that Amnesty International had now declared conditions in the camps—erupting sewers, severe malnutrition, scant medical care—"deplorable." Relief groups in the United States also criticized the British and Hong Kong governments, calling the camps "odious." Even famously neutral Canada joined in. And when one of Margaret Thatcher's attachés, the toady Mr.

Olson, proposed a plan to send back some of the refugees as a message to other Vietnamese not to attempt the journey, the Pope, from his flowery balcony above Saint Peter's, declared repatriation in this case "an assault on human dignity."

DURING THAT FIRST WEEK we went to the Wednesday night races. We ate dinner in a glassy booth high above the track. It jutted out far above the bleachers and seemed to float there, unattached to anything. It was the British club. We sat at a table with one of Albert's colleagues, a man named Kingsley, and his silent wife. He talked about the Vietnamese all night. "I do find it best," he said at one point, "that we've decided to send them back."

"We haven't decided that," Albert said. "In fact, I'm sure it won't happen. If we send them back, some will surely be hurt."

"No, no. We'll get the Viet government to agree not to touch them."

"The whole world is already against us. Even the Americans."

"Let me tell you something about the Americans," Kingsley said. "The only thing to remember is that, God bless them, they are vulgarians. The only thing they do reasonably well is entertain. They make amusing movies that the adult world indulges in for a few moments after dinner. But their political ideas? Worthless. They sympathize with

the bastards? We have forty-seven thousand of them wash-
ing up on our shore, and the Americans have offered to
take two hundred of them." He looked at me. His face was
covered in bristly gray hair. "Sorry," he said to me. Later,
when some bagpipe music came over the loudspeaker,
Kingsley leaned back and I thought he might weep.

After dinner the betting began. In the little hovering
booth the very idea of betting seemed conceptual. These
were extremely wealthy people, and money moved through
the room as if it were oxygen, or time—in such abundance
it was no longer visible.

Later Min and I took the shaky elevator to the ground
level. There I saw money. People carried it crumpled in their
hands. The cement floor was littered with slips of paper.
We watched the end of a race through an opening in the
bleachers. From above, the horses had seemed to move
effortlessly, but from here I could see the froth at their
mouths, and their eyes filling with tears as they stepped off
the track.

"Can you believe that Kingsley guy?" Min said, loos-
ening his bow tie. Bells rang, marking the start of another
race. Somebody released a bagful of white birds into the
air, for luck.

ON MONDAY, I DISCOVERED that Min's job would
be downtown, at the office, but mine would be in the
house. Early that morning I followed Albert as he limped

through a series of hallways and up some stairs, until we were walking down a long moss-green hallway. At the end of it, Albert opened a large door and introduced me to my office. It had vaulted ceilings and enormous windows that looked out over the Pacific. The sun fell in as if it were aimed directly at this room, which contained a large desk, gilded, with tiny rubies encrusted at its edges. I smiled at this room, so pleasant and dramatic simultaneously. "It's beautiful, Albert," I said. "It's so generous. I hope I won't disappoint you."

"Impossible," he said. "When Min called me from America, he said he had found a woman as serious and as beautiful as his mother. I was skeptical at first, but I see you are a remarkable woman."

I was silent at this. I had never received such a grand compliment, and I was deeply flattered. "Thank you," I finally said.

"Have a seat," he said, walking over to the desk and pulling out a chair, which was upholstered and intricately carved. I sat down. Albert sat on the edge of the desk. "As you know," he said, "Min will be married in this next year."

"That soon?" I said.

"Yes."

"Has his wife been selected?"

"No. That is where you come in. You will be choosing the wife."

"Me?"

"Yes."

"Albert, I am honored, I can't tell you how honored, but I'm really not qualified to do that. I mean, after all, I'm a foreigner here."

"You are his best friend. Who better to discover a wife?"

"Well, Min, for one."

"Min is a fool in these matters, as was I, before Lada."

"What if I choose the wrong person?"

"It's not that simple. You will actually choose a woman, and I will approve her, and then Min will meet her. He will not be required to marry her. We have all summer before you return to America, so there is plenty of time to make this decision. It must be somebody the entire family agrees upon, and since you are Lada's eyes for now, your vote will count to the same degree that hers would if she were alive."

"I don't know," I said, shaking my head.

Albert looked worried. "Of course, Sarah, if you prefer not to do this, that is fine. Please stay as our guest anyway. I do not want to drive you away with this request. I want you to be happy here."

This broke my heart. "Oh, I am," I said. "Of course I will be pleased to help you. I just hope I won't disappoint you."

"That is quite impossible," he said.

"Well, then," I said, "when should I start?"

"Now would be perfect. The applications are in the desk."

"Applications?"

"Yes. Letters and photos of different women. Some have recommended themselves; others have been recommended by their parents or friends. You will look at those, and narrow the field to perhaps fifty or one hundred that you can interview."

"What about criteria?" I asked, and winced. All those years of feminist theory had led me here, to this little red-gem room, swathed in sunlight, me sitting at a desk, asking about criteria by which I should judge other women. Hands, eyes, heart.

"I trust your instinct. The only thing I ask is that you provide a description of each woman after you meet her."

"All right."

"My own mother, Min's grandmother, sat at this same desk and determined that I would marry Lada. Her files are still in that cabinet. I've had them translated so that you can look through them."

"All right. Thank you."

"No," he said, "thank you, Sarah." He closed the door behind him.

I opened the large drawer to my left. Inside were stacks and stacks of letters. Most had a photograph clipped to them. I picked up the first one. The woman had a friendly, shy smile, and curious eyes. I thought she looked smart. I wondered briefly if this would be the one, right here. What a coincidence that would be. I read her letter. "I am a chemistry student in Beijing. I have moments of beauty. I will work, if that is your wish, or not if it isn't."

Nah, I thought, too humble for Min. I placed her application on a small table behind me, which became from that moment on the place for discarded applications. As I reached to pick up the second application, I was suddenly horrified that I had slipped into this job so easily. I stood up and went over to inspect the cabinet where Min's grandmother's notes were kept. They were neatly organized. On the front of each woman's file was Min's grandmother's assessment. She wrote in characters, and underneath, in parenthesis, somebody had translated them into English for me.

About the first woman the grandmother had written, "No, looks out of corner of eyes, suspicious and addicted to finding fault."

"Ouch," I said, flipping to the next file. Tough old broad, that grandmother. The next one said, "Possibility — Midnight-black hair, walk is like a leopard's, carnal desires strong." The next few were all rejections: "Silly, without dignity, spoils everything she touches." "Monkey-woman, scurries through the day, loves confusion." And under one name Min's grandmother had written only "Pleases no one."

I skimmed them all. There must have been close to fifty.

On the very bottom of the pile I found a description of Lada. "Is not Chinese, but of lowland Himalayas. Has no wealth, but carries purple light. Seems like a cloud about to burst. Sleeps lightly, fond of gods."

EARLY THAT EVENING, BEFORE dinner, I changed into my bathing suit and climbed the several stories of the house to spread open the large metal doors that led to the roof, into the swirling, hallucinatory light of sunset. There I found Min, sitting in a stone whirlpool, his head tilted back on the ledge, half sleeping after his first day of work.

I stared at him for a while, wondering what would happen if I offered myself as the bride. But then, as I slowly slipped into the warm water, I realized that the hundreds of hours I had spent with Min had, by the mysterious alchemy of friendship, distilled out any romance, like the stream rising all around us now, leaving us pure, fast friends.

Min's eyes opened and he smiled lazily at me.

"Min," I said, "do you have any idea what my job is?"

"I think so," he said.

"I'm supposed to find you a wife."

Min didn't look surprised but just lay there, a relaxed, confident grin on his face. "It's strange, isn't it, how things work out?"

"Yes," I said emphatically. "It's very strange."

My bedroom was next to Min's. Later that night, after we had played a gentle, courteous game of Mah-Jongg with

Albert, Min cried out in his sleep. I sat up straight in my bed. This was the second time that week. It was such a sad, childish yelping, and so deeply at odds with his personality, that it shocked me. I couldn't help thinking of his mother. I was seized with a sudden desire that she be alive and that she take on this job of finding Min happiness, finding him a wife.

Sometime in those early weeks I first saw Rapti. I often went for walks around the neighborhood late in the afternoon. I found a little shop called Asia Foodstore at the foot of the neighborhood. It was pleasantly crowded in the afternoons, full of Filipino amahs and expats shopping after work. Rapti was an amah. When I saw her, she was carrying a very large blond baby in a cloth carrier. The baby rested on her chest, facing her.

I noticed her because she was singing a quiet syncopated song to the baby, full of clicking baby noises. She had black braids and was quite tall.

Earlier that day I had found a sheet of paper on which Min's grandmother had written her definition of the "superior woman." At the top of the page is said, "Formula for Woman, According to Dignity." The formula was "Has excellent posture, which is two-thirds contentment and one-third desire."

At first I thought this a bit arbitrary. But all day the idea had been passing through my mind like a mantra. I began to think, in this strange place—half kingdom, half city—that the grandmother's formula caught the entire world in its tiny palm. *Two-thirds contentment, one-third desire.* Of course, I thought, as I spiraled my way through the trees to Asia Foodstore, that is the composition of the world. And so when I saw Rapti walking up and down the aisles, singing contentedly to the baby, letting him reach for and touch every last thing in the store, she seemed, suddenly, to embody this formula.

I ran into her almost every day after that, going up or down the hills. We nodded to each other at first, and later had small conversations. I discovered that she worked for a Canadian couple, toy-makers, who lived a block away from Min. They worked during the day and left their baby, Jack, with Rapti. "He is my best friend," Rapti said, removing her left braid from his mouth. He liked to chew on her braids whenever he could.

When I told Rapti that I was staying with the Leung family, she frowned. "Really?" she said.

"Why do you frown?"

"I hear a lot about them."

"Yes. This is a hard time for Mr. Leung and Min, his son."

"I know who Min is," she said. "I guess I don't feel too sorry for them. I feel more sorry for the Vietnamese."

I didn't say anything. I didn't want to quarrel with her.

Over the next month I discovered that she was the leader of a movement to unionize all the amahs from the

Philippines. She was also a sort of unofficial consultant to other foreign-worker groups in Hong Kong. Often when I saw her, she and the baby had returned from a rally downtown or a protest outside the Regent. They returned by bus in the late afternoon to shop at Asia Foodstore and then walk with me up the hill. The baby often leaned back in the pouch and stared up at Rapti as she talked. I liked to imagine that baby's future memories. The Canadian couple were planning on moving back home in a year, where the baby would grow up on some gentle, ordinary plain, in Alberta or Saskatchewan, and have exhilarating dreams of fantastic Asia, its red setting sun and soaring ginkgo trees, and of Rapti, too, her soft, intelligent voice, her tantalizing blue-black braids floating above.

AS THE DAYS PASSED, I slowly narrowed the list of candidates to a hundred that I would interview. I had tried to create different methods by which to sift fairly through the applications, but none was successful. Eventually I worked entirely by instinct, or, more accurately, by capricious reasoning—the tilt of her handwriting; the beauty of her name, Lily Chen, Mei-Mei Fai; or even an elaborate hairstyle I wanted to see in person.

Aside from this impossible task, I began to love my summer in Hong Kong. What had made me such a poor traveler in the past, getting no farther than Canada and once, briefly, Mexico, and disliking even that, was that I had a love of repetition and schedule. Perfect days, for me, began with identical food and drink and activity; not until dusk would I develop the restlessness that is supposed to mark people in their twenties, the desire for the day to flower, to reveal something or somebody never imagined. So in Hong Kong each weekday morning I went to the roof, sat in the whirlpool with Min, drank coffee as the sun exploded over the mountains, read the previous day's *New York Times* and the present day's *Hong Kong Standard*. We listened to BBC at eight-thirty, and when Min left for work with his father, I retired to my office to do my strange work. At noon I ate one cucumber sandwich, one bag of squid chips, and one pomelo. Then I worked until two o'clock. I spent the afternoons swimming in the pool, reading, buying groceries down at Asia Foodstore with Rapti.

Each night, though, was different from the last—horse races, restaurants that seemed carved out of pure blocks of ivory or bronze, meals of pastel lobsters as large as infants, psychedelic fireworks on the harbor. We also went to many gritty movies that were shot locally—*Hong Kong Gigolo, Warrior of the Harbor*—where in every single scene, even the most deeply romantic ones, something would explode.

But my favorite thing to do at night was to take a boat ride to the island Lantau, where we would hike in the dark jungle to a small monastery built on stone. There they served us thin soup that looked like water but tasted like the ocean—salty, warm, the smell a hint of every creature in the world—eel, fish, lizard, horse, human being—had at one time passed through it.

ALL SUMMER WE HEARD murmurs that the Hong Kong government, despite internal dissent, was actually going to attempt to repatriate some of the Vietnamese. The first group, we heard, would be sent back to Hanoi secretly and suddenly, in order to avoid riots. They would be awakened in the middle of the night and forced onto a boat or a plane.

The Vietnamese had publicly announced that they would use their homemade weapons against anybody who came for them. Relief workers and guards inside the camps reported that each night they fell asleep to the steady grinding sound of metal being sharpened into weapons.

One week in early July, Margaret Thatcher visited Hong Kong. The Vietnamese had asked that she come to the camps on her visit so that they could discuss their situation with her, but she had refused. Late on a Friday afternoon Albert took Min and me up in a small government jet to see what the Vietnamese had done to protest her refusal. The sky was cloudless, the sun a bright pink. We drank beer, circling, sweeping over the city. At first I didn't see it when Albert pointed, but then it caught the sun and sparkled. Along the silver roofs was spelled out in white stones. "Thatcher has no heart."

Albert shook his head sadly. From this distance you

could see his entire problem mapped out. In the troubled, sun-gilded water surrounding Hong Kong hundreds of people were bobbing in small boats, waiting, begging Albert and his colleagues to let them in. But if he did, they would be held in the crowded camps as illegal immigrants and treated worse than prisoners.

From here repatriation might seem to be the only answer. Min asked, "Do you think we'll end up sending them back?"

"No," Albert said. "No. I couldn't live with myself if we did that."

After the plane landed, I walked behind Min and Albert across the tarmac. I didn't want to intrude on their conversation. Watching them, I was surprised again by the severity of Albert's limp. He put his arm around Min and walked straighter. The two had a private understanding, an understanding of happiness. Each wanted the other to be happy and content, and each knew that the way to make the other happy was to be happy himself. This straining toward happiness in the midst of a difficult summer gave their home an aura of warmth and cheer, with a subtle undercurrent of sadness. Only once had I seen Albert falter in this regard. On a bright afternoon he had burst onto the roof with a letter fluttering in his hand. He handed it to Min in the whirlpool. The two men laughed and shook hands. The letter announced that they would be receiving special passports that would allow them to leave Hong Kong if things got brutal when the Chinese government took over, in 1997. Only fifty thousand families would receive these. But then, while they were congratulating each other, Albert began to choke up, and eventually he cried openly. Min leaped out of the pool and stood beside his father, patting him on his back. After his father went inside, I asked, "Why is he crying?"

"He is ashamed of his privilege."

"Hmm."

"Only a man who hates his privilege can be trusted with it."

In July, I began the interviews. Outside I could see the relentless waves of heat, but inside, cool lavender air was piped into my office. I actually enjoyed the interviews, though my method of choosing became more and more arbitrary.

A few women I could write off immediately. Some seemed too passive, others had a hostile edge, and a fair number actually asked me not to choose them, because they were doing this only to please their mothers and fathers. Most of the women I genuinely liked. One woman was so lovely that my heart skipped the moment she entered the room. One woman was unbearably funny; I met her twice, and both times I was reduced to tears of laughter. A few were such extreme overachievers at such a young age that I interviewed them very carefully, with my own

motives, looking for clues, secrets of personality. But usually my personality sketches, compared with the grandmother's, were vague and dull—"Seems nice, dignified,
beautiful, articulate."

The only time I was able even to approach the grandmother's divination and intuition was when I described my
new friend Rapti to myself. *Not Chinese*, I thought, *but
Filipino. Possesses strong heart. Loves a just God, and children. Industrious. Lives in apricot light.*

RAPTI ASKED, A GLEAM in her eye, "Have you
found a wife yet for your corrupt little Min?" It was close
to midnight. We were sitting on a large rock on a rocky
beach. Behind Asia Foodstore was a long, thin stairway
that led down through the trees to the water. I often walked
here late at night if Min went to bed early. Sometimes Rapti
joined me. She had a small Walkman that she could play
without the headphones. We'd listen to Michael Jackson
over and over and sometimes Madonna. Those two tapes,
the songs on them, still have more power and melancholy
for me than any music I've heard since. Huge pieces of
Styrofoam continually washed up in that bay, and in the
moonlight, as they rolled awkwardly through the waves,
they were florescent and beautiful.

"You know," I said, "you should meet Min. You'd really like him."

"I'm sure I wouldn't," she said.

"Perhaps we could all just meet one day, go for a walk together."

We had waded out to this rock about an hour earlier, and the tide had risen. Dead fish floated all around, studded with silver lichen, like jewelry.

"Forget it, Sarah," she said. "Even if I agreed to meet him, which I won't, you can bet your life Min would not be interested in me."

"Why not?"

"Because the Chinese hate Filipinos, the same as they hate the Vietnamese. We're either maids or their drivers."

"Min isn't like that," I said.

"If this Min is such an excellent man, why don't you fall in love with him yourself?" She looked at me provocatively, and then stood up to go, smoothing her skirt with her hands.

This suggestion startled me. "Rapti!" I said. "Of course I can't fall in love with him." I couldn't explain that the way I felt about Min was the same way I felt about her. I looked up at her. Her hair, not in its usual braids, whipped around. I felt a stab of longing. I liked everything about her. When she spoke, she was funny and smart. She was strong; I had seen her throw the huge baby into the air and catch him easily. And when she fell silent, as now, staring over the bay in the direction of her cluster of islands, I couldn't help wondering and wanting to know exactly what she was thinking.

A COUPLE OF WEEKS later, as Min and I stood in line for a movie, I said, "Min, you would consider marrying someone of a different nationality, wouldn't you?"

"Absolutely," he said. "I am of mixed heritage myself."

"Good," I said. "I want you to meet a friend I have made."

"A friend?"

"Rapti, the woman I told you about who works down the street?"

"The amah? The Filipino amah?"

"Yes," I said defensively.

Min had his hands in his pockets. He rocked back and forth on his heels. It was a cool, breezy night. The couple in front of us in line were silent, and they seemed to be waiting for Min's answer as well.

"Well, it's really just not done," Min said.

"What do you mean?"

"The Chinese and the Filipinos have a bitter history," he said. "It would be a lot to overcome."

"Rapti would say it was prejudice, not animosity."

"Perhaps," he admitted.

"But you will meet her?" I said.

"Of course I will meet any friend of yours. But Sarah, really, you don't need to take this job seriously. It's a formality, that's all."

"I know," I said. "I just want you to meet her. We could all be friends."

But throughout the movie I was planning the meeting place. The grandmother had written in her notes, "Himalayan Lada will meet Albert in meadowland. Quiet enough for the future to be seen. Sky of birds. Sage moss and high willows, and a house that has not been entered for over one hundred years."

AT THE END OF August, at the close of the rainy season and one week before I was to return to America, a fight broke out at the camp Chi Ma Wan when Hong Kong police went in to check for weapons. The Vietnamese had carved spears out of tent pegs, and knives from metal bed slats. They stoned the police, until the police retaliated with a tear gas whose concentration blinded several children. Fourteen Vietnamese were seriously injured, and one was dead. When news of this spread to other camps, seven Vietnamese men in different camps disemboweled themselves in protest.

As this occurred, I was writing, in a careful yet uninspired calligraphy, the names of the seven women I thought most appropriate for Min to consider for marriage. I wasn't by any means satisfied that my choices were significantly more appropriate than the others, but I was relieved to have finished the job. As for Rapti, she still refused to meet Min.

That night I was dreaming of Min when he actually appeared above me, peering down into my face. "Sarah," he said, "wake up. Dad hasn't come home yet; it's already one a.m."

"Yeah?" I said, still too nearly asleep to guess what that might mean.

"I think tonight's the night."

"The night?"

"I think they're going back tonight."

"To Hanoi?" I said.

"Yes. I think we should go to the airport."

"Okay." I sat up.

"We have no car."

"I'll call Rapti."

"Ah, the stubborn Rapti," he said, and smiled.

Rapti picked us up in the Canadians' car. I got in the front seat and Min got in the back. He reached his hand forward to Rapti. "At last we meet," he said.

"Hello," she said, smiling, shaking her head, and then she gunned the car into reverse, out of the long, curving driveway.

The drive to Kai Tak airport took about fifteen minutes, exactly enough time for Min and Rapti to move from a polite, vague disagreement into a full-scale argument.

"So, your father is sending the refugees back tonight? Did he get an agreement that they won't be maltreated back home?"

"Well, first of all," Min said from the backseat, "my father does not want to send them back. You'll see when we get there. He will be opposing the action, at the expense of his own job."

"Really?" Rapti said. "I find that hard to believe. Considering."

"Considering what?"

"Considering his past record with the refugees."

"Are you referring to his fight for reforms within the camps?"

"I'm referring to the fact that he proposed a policy to *fine* them for having children inside the camps. Some of them have lived there for years. It's very cruel."

I looked at Min. "It happened while we were in the States," he said, and then he turned to Rapti and said, "All he meant was that having children during these crisis months would place a strain on the community."

"Strain on the community—that's a ridiculous argument. Then nobody in the world should have children. I think asking people not to have children is just another form of genocide."

After a moment of silence Rapti looked at me and shrugged. *Sorry,* she mouthed. I looked back at Min, who made his eyes as big as possible and then shook his head in amazement.

When we arrived at the airport, the Vietnamese were in the process of boarding the plane. We got as close as we could and stood on a little grassy patch, which I thought was sadly reminiscent of a meadow, at the edge of the runway. We stared through the barbed wire. Albert in fact wasn't protesting. He was standing at the foot of the plane's staircase, bowing to each person who stepped onto the stairs.

The time for protest was past, apparently, and now he could only apologize to each of them, even the smallest children. Some of the people shouted at him, a few spit, and a couple even lunged for him. I saw one refugee bow back, though, and the two men, head to head, looked like foreign dignitaries caught in a dreadful, unlikely situation. I remembered that Albert had said to me once that a person must bow even if he doesn't want to. He must bow at everything, and the more he doesn't want to bow, the more he must. He recalled a phrase that went, "The forehead should be rough with bowing."

The air was heavy and humid, with an odor of overripe flowers. Overhead two helicopters hovered, churning the air, lifting my outer clothes an inch off my body. A dark rain started to fall.

Finally a break in the line occurred as a mother knelt to talk to her child, who was hysterical. Albert turned and saw us. His face was streaming with tears. He smiled though, and bowed to us. Min bowed back, and then I bowed, and then Rapti herself bowed to him. She had a stern look on her face, and I could tell that she did not approve of this but that she recognized the complexity of Albert's situation.

If I had been able, like Min's grandmother, to read the

gestures of women, to discern their entire nature and future in one movement of a head or hand, I would have seen, as Rapti bowed, the present picture open for one moment to reveal the future—a warm, gently decorated apartment in a skyscraper high above a city that belongs again to the Chinese, who have carried it into the twenty-first century by transforming it into an even higher and wealthier and stranger city. On the crowded streets below, the Vietnamese, once held in the camps, have penetrated the bloodstream of the city, so that they are the ones deciding which new refugees to accept and which to reject.

And asleep, sprawled like a starfish on the floor of the apartment, is a small boy with a boxy, bold, contented face, his features drawn from such a wide circle of Asia that one can almost see the rays extending from him to all his origins—from the Philippines to the edges of Russia and Inner Mongolia, across the Tibetan plateau, into the foothills of the Himalayas, touching even the upper lip of India.

But for now none of that was revealed. In fact, as the three of us stood in the perfumey rain of Asia, watching Albert's desperate, endless bowing and what must have been the unbearable desire and longing of the refugees, I couldn't bring myself to believe that the balance of the world—two-thirds contentment, one-third desire—could ever be restored.

WORLD PARTY

▼ ▼ ▼

ONE

It was always this moment in the fall semester, toward the end, the days shorter and darker, the seedpods and leaves broken and beautifully spent across our campus, that I brought out my lecture on Ovid. You don't have to do much with Ovid—just begin to read and every person in the room gets spoken to about the deepest matters in their life. *My intention is to tell of bodies changed to different forms: The gods, who made the changes, will help me—or so I hope—with a poem that runs from the world's beginning to our own days.*

My period was Roman Antiquity, and this class was a

survey course, so we had already run through Cleopatra, Caesar, and Virgil, now to Ovid. I usually ended with Jesus, when time itself cleaved in two, and the soul was united with God, infinity making its way into our battered little sphere of finity.

This was a late morning class, so even as I lectured, I was going over the afternoon in my mind: meet with Terrance in the faculty lounge, walk with him to committee meeting, and then get to World Party by five. World Party was a little banquet my son's school put on for the students. It was a Quaker alternative to Halloween; all the children dressed up as characters from history or books or their own imagination, while the parents laid out food before them in a great banquet, the theme being that everyone, every last person, is invited to the banquet. My son, Teddy, was seven, so this would be our third World Party. I looked forward to it every year, despite the inevitable run-in with my ex-husband and his new family.

World Party always brought to mind a sermon I'd heard long ago, in Riverside Church in New York City. I was in my twenties at the time and the preacher kept repeating these words, for possibly two or three full minutes—*You don't think you're invited to the banquet? Well, you are. You don't think you're invited to the banquet? It couldn't be you. Well, you are.*

Partway through my lecture, I heard some shouting and anxious merrymaking outside, but it didn't occur to

me that it was a serious crowd gathering, despite the jan-
gly, exciting energy to it. In the early part of the century,
when this university was being built, some intelligent and
benevolent architect or planner had put the history building right on the quad, a vast, beautiful, ever-changing
landscape that would be the home of the many protests
down through the years. During the sixties this classroom
was a theater overlooking an endless stream of protests,
mostly against the war. And now, in the fall of 1981, there
seemed to be a resurgence of protest activity—against sex-
ism, against apartheid, against a cement plant being built
on the edge of campus, against every single tree that was
taken down to clear way for more buildings, and against
various faculty members for their fascism or their commu-
nism or their support for Third-World dictators.

My favorite agitators were the streakers, who always
looked so dramatic and vulnerable and innocent to me.
They were always tall skinny men, their nakedness not
sexual at all, but more like a great, comical symbol of hu-
manity. Their whole message was wrapped up in the image,
Christ-like, absurd.

Today the weather was supporting the unease; it was
dark for daytime, and the wind was shifting about. Also,
the campus was alive with a general unrest in those days,
as the university was considering suspending the activity
of one of the most visible protest groups on campus. The
group went by the name Harvest. Their faculty advisor

was a man named Stewart Applebaum. In fact, my meeting later today was an emergency meeting to discuss what to do with Stewart Applebaum and his band of protestors, whom I admired, actually, but also I understood there was something frightening about the cult aspect of the group, their devotion to each other, their extremism, their seeming almost dionysian happiness when they gathered. Stewart Applebaum was an economics professor, so a lot of the group's time seemed to be taken up probing the university's investments, looking for scurrilous, immoral places the university was making money. They had built shanties in the quad when it was discovered the university was still supporting apartheid financially; they chained themselves to trees that had been tagged for destruction to make way for a new administration building. And they held endless, vigilant demonstrations against a cement plant that was to be built on the edge of campus and would pollute the campus pretty much permanently.

I had always considered them a force for good on campus, a reasonable way for students to learn the art of dissent, and a sort of exciting, ever-present challenge to the status quo, which I thought was healthy. But then lately, their protests had taken on a sort of worrisome cast. It had been discovered that three of the young men were proposing a hunger strike set to start two days hence, and this had seized all the university administrators, and everybody actually, with a kind of terror.

TWO

After class, I swung by our main office to pick up a big stack of applications for our graduate program. The students applying each had to write an essay on a moment in history that interested them. Our graduate program was very popular on account of two professors mostly. There was Jonathan Rudd, who was writing a history of the whole world told through one historical figure from each half-century. The books were written as a series, and he had completed nearly twelve of them. Some historians scoffed at them a little, but they were best sellers, and actually I found them really entertaining. Our other best seller was Sylvia Nixon, who had written one very beautiful, slightly annoying book—a memoir essentially—that somehow interposed the events of her life with some of the greatest events of the twentieth century. You couldn't even call her a historian, really. She used history in the most chilling way possible, as a metaphor for events in her own life.

And then I headed, as every day, back to our shabby little coffee-Xerox room to find my friend Liv, just returned from her Italy 1912 class. Liv's area was Italian Fascism, heavy emphasis on Mussolini, who was cut from the same cloth as Liv's tyrannical father. Liv had emerged from a terrible childhood and early marriage to be always the sanest, most stable, most cheerful person in any room. Every day after teaching we retired here, to this little notch in the wall, which we just called "small room." Our faculty mail-boxes were in here, so every now and then one of the men in our department would duck in, chat a bit, and retrieve his mail, but they knew the room was ours. One had even complained about it, said he didn't appreciate having to get his mail out of the "ladies room" every day.

Liv was standing at the narrow window. We were on the third floor, and our view faced away from campus: You could spot, in the far distance, a patch of something we knew to be the ocean. It was a like a little painting—a min-iature line of pine trees, a procession to the sea. Today some dark blue and gray clouds were roiling around, carrying something gorgeous and frightening in from the ocean. Liv was dressed in an old corduroy Laura Ashley dress, which looked like it would be worn by the school teacher in *Little House on the Prairie*. She was staring outside, pensively. "A storm is blowing from Paradise," she said, quoting Walter Benjamin.

I saw she had an application in her hand; she'd already begun reading. "How are they?" I asked.

"They're good, they're fine. Though the one I'm read-ing right now is about Ronald Reagan's presidency, which isn't quite in the past yet. It's hard to classify it historically already."

"We should have a department called the Present," I said.

"The Department of the Present," Liv said. "It would

be about what one did last night, this morning, and what one will do tonight," Liv said.

"They would all major in it," I said, as Terrance appeared in the doorway.

"Oh we're all having lunch?" Liv said. Terrance had originally been her friend; he was in the Biology Department and had consulted with her while working on his book, which had just been published and was a completely riveting history of various plagues—viral and bacterial—that had flourished on earth in the bodies of men, women, and children from approximately 200,000 BC until now, October of 1981. It was called *Plagues and People* and seemed to have no preference for the people over the plagues. In fact, at times in the narrative he seemed to be meditating quite deeply on the plight of this or that virus, as it desperately tried to survive on the human body, having to feed off it, but also having to tread carefully so as not to kill its fragile host.

Then last September Terrance and I had been put on a committee together—the Faculty Hearings Committee—so he and I had spent many Friday afternoons cloistered in a little room high atop the campus, pondering various faculty misdeeds.

"We can't have lunch," I said to Liv. "Terrance and I have an emergency meeting for Stewart Applebaum."

"That's today?" she said.

"It's today. It's in an hour," I said.

"Okay. Geesh," she said. "I wish I could come along. Good luck. It's getting so scary."

"I hope we find that he's innocent and that the whole thing is just getting away from him."

"I don't think you'll find that," Liv said. "I think you'll find that he's the devil. Like, the real devil. Using young people's passions against them, and for his own purposes."

"What are the chances that the actual devil is on our faculty?" Terrance seemed thrilled at the thought.

"I think it's likely," Liv said. "Justine has met him already, you know," she said to Terrance, gesturing to me. "She found him attractive."

"Ooooh," Terrance said. "I can't wait to meet him."

"It's a hearing," I said, "I don't think you'll really *meet* him, exactly."

"Well, we can still make eyes at him," said Terrance.

I had met Stewart Applebaum about a month earlier, at a library benefit, and had been surprised by what a cheerful, relaxed person he was. I'd expected someone darkly muttering, or angry, or a blowhard of some sort. But he had been actually really charming and fun. And I was still clinging (pathetically) to a little thing he said to me, that we ought to have coffee one day together. I had even mentioned it to Liv, hoping she could help me scrutinize it for any romantic content.

"Couldn't you tell by the way he said it?" she had asked.

"Not really. I mean, normally I would think yes, but it just seems so unlikely. He's about ten years younger than me."

"Some brave women overcome that."

"You have to be really on top of your game."

"Yes. You've got to keep it all together."

What had struck me about that night was the sudden return of an old feeling, what Rilke called the "calling to vast things." I had been so involved in the march of time—my marriage, Teddy's birth, his troubles, my work, my divorce—that I'd forgotten this feeling entirely. I was stepping back inside the library from its big balcony, which is held by huge white pillars and whose view is the entire hissing, southern campus, with the deep turbulent ocean visible in the distance. Stewart Applebaum and I had just had a brief conversation, mostly about some work a colleague of mine was doing on the various economies of Central America, and we had already said goodbye, but then he said to me as I was walking away, *We should have coffee sometime soon.* I realized it wasn't the most stunning suggestion any man has said to any woman, but it so genuinely surprised me that it was as if the feeling itself—of attraction or whatever—just appeared as a person appears. I was like a woman at a drawer, putting away her party dresses between tissue paper, and there he stood in the doorway—not Stewart Applebaum, but this feeling—gentlemanly, feral, breathtaking, peaceful, something very close to life itself, asking me for one more dance down in the meadow.

THREE

The meeting was across campus. Since the day was so blustery, there was a strange, exciting, hurricaney feel to it, and as we stepped into the quad, a wind was whipping around some tiny raindrops. In one corner some students were setting up a makeshift stage and there was a disorganized crowd gathering. Their signs were face down on the ground to prevent the rain from wrecking them, so we couldn't read what they would be protesting. I suspected it was Stewart Applebaum's group but wasn't sure until I heard a young man shout out as he walked under the clocktower, "While in life," and a couple guys working on the sound stage stood up and called back, "To fight for life." These were references to a Stephen Spender poem that the group used as a call and response. It was a beautiful poem—"I Think Continually of Those Who Were Truly Great," which was written in 1942.

"So it's them," I said to Terrance.

"Yes. I guess they may be protesting the hearing itself."

"Yes."

Early in the semester, our chancellor, who was quite sick with a rare form of late-stage leukemia but still working, suggested in a way I found plaintive and sweet, especially from a man so close to death, that perhaps the students should use these "gatherings" not as a time to protest but rather to celebrate what they appreciated about their country and their university, and this had enraged the students and sent them spiraling into the quad with signs aloft protesting the chancellor himself.

I had one quick detour before the meeting, as Teddy's teacher had sent home a little note asking us to bring along a "healthy dessert" to World Party tonight. So Terrance accompanied me to Moon's, a tiny cozy convenience store on the edge of campus, run by Mr. Moon and his wife Liliane. They had Fig Newtons, which I knew were not exactly healthy but they were faintly educational and maybe even sort of biblical. And anyway, I was in the habit of just setting the food down quickly and then disowning it entirely, even in my own mind. And since my ex-husband, Ted, and his wife, Elizabeth, and their two little children—a beautiful blond fairy family—would be there, it would be important not to place my package of cookies anywhere near Elizabeth's offering, which would be something homey and exquisite, lemon squares or warm flaxen oatcakes.

We had about five minutes to get to the meeting after we exited Moon's. As I was telling Terrance about my newest concerns about Teddy— he was refusing to dress up as a character from a book for the party tonight and instead wanted to dress up as death, or a disease, or a rat—I saw that across Great Lawn, the white clover flowers had sprung up everywhere, ten thousand of them. It was my favorite sight—the field suddenly white instead of green.

"Well, he's testing the hypothesis," Terrance said. "Is it a World Party or not? Is everything really invited?"

"I guess," I said. "Maybe. I just wish he wanted to be Willy Wonka or something."

"Well, what is he going to be after all?"

"We compromised with a black hole. He's going to be a black hole."

Just the night before, the Nobel Prize had gone to the Bulgarian writer Elias Canetti for his book *Crowds and Power*, which I happened to have read (crowds as wildfire, crowds as birds, crowds as a hillside of trees), but it was a lesser play of his—called *Their Days Are Numbered*—that I recall when I think back to that day, walking across the wildish, newly white field with Terrance. In the play, every person wears a medallion with the day, month, and year of their death on it, so that you know while talking to somebody when it is they will die. I don't know what I would have done differently if I'd known how soon Terrance would die. I suppose clutch his arm, and stay close to him, try to see things a little longer his way, which was generous and serious, but I was already doing that, holding on to his muscley, tattooed arm.

As we were making our way up the stairs I saw Stewart Applebaum just standing there, waiting for his time to go in and appear before us. "Oh hey," I said to him. "It's you," he said. Terrance smiled and opened the door for us both.

FOUR

Of all the college committees, this one — the Faculty Hearings Committee — was the greatest. If a faculty member did anything suspect — threatened the dean with a gun, gave their classes all A's, denied the Holocaust — it was referred to us, the most unskilled tribunal ever assembled.

When Terrance and I arrived, Dana Fisher, our committee chair, who looked like maybe a handsome Ichabod Crane with a salt-and-pepper mustache, was already there seated at the table, behind which there was a big window letting on to an enormous, two-hundred-year-old oak tree. All of our deliberations over the past two years had taken place in the measured, gorgeous aura of this tree. It had turned in the last few days a bright and otherworldly bronze.

Dana, who was a nonvoting member of the committee, had laid out at each of our places a little packet of information about Applebaum including, strangely, a big glossy picture of him, as if we were considering him for a part in a movie. In the photo, Applebaum looked serious but kind, handsome in a dark, feathered-hair sort of way. His CV was there too: BA from Berkeley, MA from Wharton, PhD in economics from the University of Michigan.

Within moments, our last member, Geraldine, arrived, bearing poppy seed muffins. Geraldine was a formidable woman — brave, ethereal, intelligent, tall, fragile, and frequently contemptuous of our committee. She was already in her sixties, and had been in that first wave of feminists who had to be absolute warriors.

Dana decided to invite Applebaum into the meeting right from the start, so he could help us understand the situation, before we began our deliberations. When Applebaum entered he apologized quickly to us all, for taking away our Friday afternoon.

Dana was a Quaker, so ran our meetings in an atmosphere of almost total silence, out of which speech was supposed to arise like a revelation of some sort. So we all sat quietly for a while, looking over the materials. Finally, Dana said, "We have a crisis. We have a young student in the hospital, after refusing to eat for three days, and we have two more following in his footsteps. They are members of this group, Harvest."

"What specifically are they protesting?" Terrance asked Applebaum.

"Well, we've discovered that one of our board members— Dean Forenter, in fact—is the head of a waste company that is currently violating state regulations and dumping waste every day in a waterway that feeds into the Atlantic. These boys cannot tolerate that."

"Did you instruct them to strike?" Geraldine asked. I could tell she was angry.

"No. But we frequently talk about nonviolent means to protest."

"But this is quite violent," I said. "It's a type of terrorism. It's a method of force."

"I suppose. But for me the question is always whether it matches the activity it is meant to address. We've been reading A. S. Mill, *The Uses of Obedience and Disobedience,* as well as some old Emerson essays. The students who are involved in this particular action are intelligent, free-thinking adults. I don't tell them what to do. One of them—Griffith Tran—has been studying quite carefully the essays of—"

"Forgive me," I said, "but you sound supportive of what they are doing."

"Let me put it this way," he said. "I will be happy if they stop, but I can't help but be proud of them."

"Hmmm," Dana said. And we all fell silent again for awhile.

My mind was passing back and forth promiscuously between the matter at hand and a deep inner discussion on the difference in Applebaum's age and mine. If you squinted we were almost the same age. We were of the same generation, at least. He was thirty-five to my forty-four, which I couldn't decide if it was vast or negligible. We were on earth at the same time, and maybe that's all that mattered. Still, how would it all go? I would be fifty when he was forty-one, which would be okay I guess, but then I would be sixty when he was fifty-one, when he could still conceivably date, for instance, a thirty-five-year-old, which would put me at sixty in competition with women in their thirties. *Forget it!* Dana was going over some by-laws, while I suffered through my breakup with Applebaum fifteen years hence.

Geraldine leaped in. "You keep referring to these students as 'adults,' " which I think is your unconscious way of removing yourself from any responsibility. Anybody who has had a child of that age knows that they are hardly functioning with the same judgment they will hold in the future when they are thirty and forty."

"Well," Applebaum said, "they are more passionate, yes, and energetic. But I've found that people at that age can have a kind of intuitive sense of justice that disappears after people's lives take on more responsibilities to their children and to their communities."

"But the power differential seems to escape you," Geraldine said. "You have power over them whether you choose to acknowledge it or not."

It was three p.m. and the day was already getting darker. There was no rain but an intense afternoon darkness. The tree outside our window registered this by getting brighter, turning its inner light up, and its wet, golden leaves shook with delight at all this weather. My thoughts ran to Teddy and to World Party. I was not late yet, but darkness always signaled to me that I had to get to Teddy, wherever he was. He had a little tic that deepened as the day progressed, and if he got tired especially. Not that it seemed to bother him. We almost never spoke of it. I didn't want to make him self-conscious. But then I worried that by not mentioning it, I was ignoring something that was distressing him, or just leaving him to manage something on his own when I should be accompanying him in some way.

When I was young, my family often spent weekends at our old family homestead up in Southern Saskatchewan. Every Sunday we went to a small, beautiful Lutheran church, whose pastor had a severe tic that ran all the way from his temple down across his left cheekbone, over his jaw, down his neck, affecting even his left shoulder. The tic occurred every thirty or so seconds, without fail. You could have timed the passage of the sun and moon with it. And to this day I can't hear any of those old Bible stories—the exile from Eden, Noah's flood, the binding of Isaac, Jesus on Calvary—without picturing and even feeling in my own face that great quake, that grave, magnificent revelation of fragility. His name was Glademacher, and he had a beautiful old man's face, God and time and mortality working its way over it.

By the time we all stepped out, two hours later, we each—Terrance, Geraldine, and I—had a tiny slip of paper in our pockets, with yes and no written on it. We were to check the box beside yes or no, regarding whether we should allow Applebaum to continue to direct Harvest. A no vote meant that Harvest should be disbanded immediately. We had to return this to a little mailbox outside this building by 6:30 tonight. I was pretty sure Geraldine would check no, they shouldn't be allowed to continue, and Terrance would check yes, they should of course be allowed to continue, to let everybody's destinies play out as they will. So that left me.

FIVE

The Quaker Day School was so cozy, I just wanted to curl up in the reading corner, on its huge alphabet pillows, and read away into the night, the wind and rain swirling all around. Maybe *The Borrowers,* or some Beverly Cleary. Of all the books I've read since childhood, of all the civilizations risen and fallen, none of them described the futility and fun of life so accurately as *The Jumblies,* by the great epileptic and depressive Edward Lear, the twentieth child of his parents.

> *They went to sea in a Sieve they did,*
> *In a Sieve they went to sea:*
> *In spite of all their friends could say,*
> *On a winter's morn, on a stormy day,*
> *In a Sieve they went to sea.*

The parents, all of us soaking wet, battered, nearly ruined by our days, crowded around the outside of the room and watched the quiet processional of children to the banquet table, which was laid with quince, pomegranates, squash, lemonade. My Fig Newtons were actually turning out to be quite appropriate. The teacher, Dominique, had swiftly arranged them in a complicated circle/maze design around a huge platter. She was a magician, who took all of life into her and there transformed it into something that a seven-year-old would love.

The children were solemn at first — Mother Earth with her elaborate headdress, Daffy Duck, a Moon and a Star, a Lightbulb, and then Teddy, with his cape of nothing. Dominique had us all bow our heads and then she said this little Quaker nonprayer based on an Emily Dickinson poem: "Who comes to dine must bring his feast, or find the banquet mean. The banquet is not laid without till it is laid within."

Ted was across the room from me, with Elizabeth and their two toddlers. Elizabeth waved. Ted didn't *not* wave. It just didn't occur to him that we should wave at each other. He had a little bit of Teddy's efficiency with emotion, or maybe inability. It actually made me love Ted, too, a little. He had an animal's straightforward relationship to life, though, as with Teddy, this was coupled with a genuine, very interesting, and companionable intelligence. Still, I worried, basically every second of every day, about Teddy, who seemed farther out on the limb than his father. For instance, the banquet table was kidney shaped, with a big bulge at one end, and then a slim curve, with a tiny bulge at the other end. Teddy was down there, alone. The other children were jostling with each other, laughing, smiling, arguing, and Teddy was sitting there by himself, thinking and eating. Nobody seemed to notice but me — it was just a natural configuration to them, like the inevitable placement of stars in the sky.

I knew for a fact that Teddy wasn't thinking about it — he would be thinking about subtraction, or Fibonacci, or maybe about the Hilbert Hotel, which was a hotel with an infinite number of rooms to which an infinite amount of guests kept appearing and asking for rooms. This was a thought experiment that there were whole books written about, and whole careers devoted to.

Still, the sight of him — a black hole at the end of the table alone — made me almost unbearably sad. I went to crouch down in the crook of the table and talk to him. "How are you, Teddy?" I tried to close the distance between Teddy and the other kids, chatting with the little girl Betsy Charter, Mother Nature, about her feathers and the jewels in her headdress. I suppose I looked ludicrous, trying to horn in on the World Party. But I didn't care. I'd sit there forever. In my mind I'd sit there all night, and into tomorrow and the weekend, trying to bridge the gap between Teddy and everybody else.

But it ended, thankfully, within the hour, and we were on our way. Back to campus, where I still needed to place my vote. Teddy and I walked across those same white fields of clover, and just the thought of Terrance even existing (he was out at a restaurant with his lawyer love right now), casting his generous eye on everything—*he's testing the hypothesis*—made me happy to be alone with Teddy again, thinking about everything.

"So if the Hilbert Hotel can accommodate any subsets of infinity, like busfuls of new people, infinite busfuls of new people, then there are different types of infinity. There are subsets of infinity," Teddy said.

"Yes. Apparently they finally proved that."

"The Hilbert Hotel proves it."

"Yes."

I'd had this conversation with Teddy many times, and each time I found myself wondering if anybody except a mother would find his austere intelligence companionable. When I think back on my childhood and young adulthood it seems the whole enterprise was awash with attempting to understand other people and get them to understand you, loving them and getting them to love you. Teddy's path would be so different from that: I couldn't even quite imagine it. He just didn't care about that. He was alone with the Alone.

The one sermon I'd never heard and needed now, needed every day of Teddy's life, was regarding Abraham and Isaac. But who can bear it? Who could bear to speak of it—Abraham, one of the kindest, most soulful characters in the Bible, being asked to carry his beloved only child, Isaac, up Moriah, where the child would be sacrificed. The story is made doubly terrifying because of Isaac's innocence and trust in his father. But the Bible is clear; children will have a destiny, and they will have a mountain, and all you can do is accompany them with the terrible knowledge of all the difficulties they will encounter. They skip beside you, or in Teddy's case, they walk carefully through the wildflowers, dreaming of infinity.

So at the end of the day, with Teddy beside me, I slipped a little yes vote into the mailbox. Everybody would just have to live with that.

FIALTA

▼ ▼ ▼

From where I stand, on the bridge overlooking the Chicago River, the city looks like a strange but natural landscape, as if it arises as surely and inevitably from the hands of life as does a field of harvest wheat or a stand of red firs. After all, the city was designed by country boys—Mies van der Rohe, Burnham and Root, Frank Lloyd Wright, Louis Sullivan—all wild and dashing, dreaming up the city in the soft thrum of the countryside.

But the buildings that most reflect nature, at least midwestern nature, in all its dark and hidden fertility, are those by Franklin Stadbakken, the so-called architect of the prairies, that great and troubled mess of a man I once knew.

THREE YEARS AGO, WHEN I was a senior at Northwestern, I sent Stadbakken a packet of drawings and a statement of purpose. Every year Stadbakken chooses five apprentices to come live with him on the famous grounds of Fialta, his sprawling workshop, itself an architectural dream rising and falling over the gentle hills of southwestern Wisconsin. My sketches were of skyscrapers, set down with a pencil on pale blue drafting paper. They'd been drawn late in the night, and I knew hardly anything about how to draw a building, except that it ought not to look beautiful; it ought to be spare and slightly inaccessible, its beauty only suggested, so that a good plan looked like a secret to be passed on and on, its true nature hidden away.

Two months later I received back a letter of acceptance. At the bottom of the form letter there was a note from Stadbakken himself that read, "In spite of your ambition, your hand seems humble and reasonable. I look forward to your arrival."

I had been reading, off and on, that year, a biography of Stadbakken, and this moment when I read his handwriting was one of the most liberating in my life—in fact, so much so it was almost haunting, as if a hand had leapt out of the world of art—of books and dreams—and pulled me in.

MY FIRST EVENING AT Fialta was referred to as orientation but was really a recitation by one of the two second-year apprentices, named Reuben, of What Stadbakken

Liked, which was, in no particular order, mornings, solitude, black coffee, Yeats, order, self-reliance, privacy, skits, musicals, filtered light, thresholds, lightning. "Piña coladas," the woman sitting beside me—Elizabeth—said quietly. "Getting caught in the rain."

"Fialta," Reuben continued, "is dedicated not to the fulfillment of desire but to the transformation of desire into art." We were sitting in the commons, a beautiful, warm room that doubled as our dining room, our office, and our lounge. There was an enormous fireplace, windows streaming with slanted and dying light, and a big wooden table, whose legs were carved with the paws of beasts at the floor. There was a golden shag carpet and stone walls. It was high up, and the views were spectacular, but the room was intimate. So this statement regarding desire seemed almost heartbreakingly Freudian, since the room and all of Fialta, with its endless private corners and stunning walkways and fireplaces, seemed to ask you at every turn to fall in love, yet that was the one thing that was not permitted. Reuben went on to say, "Stadbakken does not tolerate well what he calls overfraternization. He sees it as a corruption of the working community if people, well. . . ." And there was a nervous moment. Reuben seemed to have lost his footing. Nobody knew what to say until a tall woman in the back, whose name would turn out to be Indira Katsabrahmanian, and whose beauty would turn out to be the particular rocks on which Reuben's heart would be dashed, spoke up: "*Sodo-sudu.*" Reuben raised his eyebrows at her. "Fool around," she said, with a slightly British accent. "It means to not fool around."

Reuben nodded.

So, no love affairs. As soon as this was declared, it was as if a light had turned on in the room. Until this point, everyone had been so focused on the great absent man himself and his every desire that nobody had really looked around that carefully. But at this mention that we could not fall in love, we all turned to see who else was there. Each person seemed suddenly so interesting, so vital, a beautiful portal through which one might pass, secretly. And this was when I saw Sands, who was, with Reuben, returning for her second year at Fialta. When I try to call forth my first impression of Sands, it is so interpreted by the light of loss that what I see is somebody already vanishing, but beautifully, into a kind of brightness. And as Stadbakken's beloved Yeats said of Helen, how can I blame her, being what she was and Fialta being what it is?

As we left that evening, I talked briefly to Reuben and to Elizabeth, whose nickname became Groovy in those few moments, owing to her look, which had a hundred implications—of Europe and Asia, of girls, of tough guys, of grannies. And I then fell in step beside Sands as she walked outside. It was slightly planned on my part, but not entirely, which allowed me to think that the world was a little bit behind me and my desire. It was mid-September, and in this part of the country there were already ribbons of wintry cold running through the otherwise mild evenings. We had a brief, formal conversation. We discussed Fialta, then Chicago. I had thought I was walking her home, but it seemed that we were actually, suddenly, winding up a pathway toward Stadbakken's living quarters.

"Oh," I said. "Where are we going?"

"I'm going up to check on him." She pointed way up to a sort of lighthouse circling above us.

"Stadbakken?"

"Yes." There was light pouring out the window.

"Oh sure, go ahead," I said.

She smiled at me and then walked off. And I turned to walk back to my room, slightly horrified at myself. *Go ahead,* I repeated to myself. *Oh, hey, go ahead.* This is the whole problem with words. There is so little surface area to reveal whom you might be underneath, how expansive and warm, how casual, how easygoing, how cool, and so it all comes out a little pathetic and awkward and choked.

As I walked home, I turned back and saw through the trees again that window, ringing with clarity and light above the dark grounds, the way the imagination shines above the dark world, as inaccessible as love, even as it casts its light all around.

THAT EVENING I LAY in bed reading Christopher Alexander, the philosopher-king of architects: "The fact is, that this seeming chaos which is in us is a rich, rolling, swelling, dying, lilting, singing, laughing, shouting, crying, sleeping order." I paused occasionally to stare out the large window beside my bed, which gave way to the rolling hills, toward Madison's strung lights, and, had I the eyes to see, my hometown of Chicago burning away in the distance. Reuben knocked on my door. We were roommates, sharing a large living room and kitchen. Reuben was the cup full to the brim, and maybe even a little above the brim but without spilling over, as Robert Frost put it. If one of the skills of being properly alive is the ability to contain gracefully one's desires, then Reuben was the perfect living being.

"I forgot to give you your work assignment," he said.

The literature on Fialta I received over the summer had mentioned grounds work, which I had assumed meant carpentry or landscaping, but now Reuben informed me that I would be in charge of the cows and the two little pigs.

"There are animals here?"

"Yes. Down in the barn."

"There's a barn?"

"Yes. At the end of the pasture."

"Of course," I said.

He was already bowing out of the door when I asked what I was to do with them.

"Milk the cows, feed the pigs," he said, and ducked out.

I should never have sent in those skyscrapers, I thought to myself as I fell asleep. Those are what got me the cow assignment. You can feel it as you sketch plans, the drag in the hand, the worry, the Tower of Babel anxiety as the building grows too high. There ought not to be too much hubris in a plan. But this is not a simple directive either, since a plan also needs to be soaring and eccentric and confident. But still humble. A perfect architect might be like a perfect person, the soul so correctly aligned that it can ascend with humility. Humble and dashing, those two things, always and forever.

YOU COULD SAY THAT Fialta was not quite in its prime. Its reputation was fading a little, and all its surfaces tarnishing, but so beautifully that Fialta was a more romantic place than it must have been even at the height of its influence, something that could be said of Stadbakken as well. Early success as an architect and a slide into some obscurity had given his reputation a kind of legendary, old-fashioned quality, even though he was only in his late fifties. At seven o'clock, at the dimming of the next day, he stepped into the commons for our first session. He had the looks of a matinee idol in the early twilight of his career, and he seemed more substantially of the past than anybody I've ever met, so that even now, when I remember him, it is in black and white. He is wistful in my memory, staring off, imagining a building that might at last equal nature— generative and wild, but utterly organized at the heart.

That night in the commons, Stadbakken entered and

said only this: "We have a new project. It's what we were all hoping for. It's a theater, along a city block in Chicago, surrounded on two sides by a small park designed by Olmsted. I'd like the theater to think about the park."

Sands and Reuben nodded, so the rest of us did as well. "Yes, well," he said, "you might as well begin." He put his hands together, in a steeple, as he stared at us—Reuben, Sands, me, Indira, and Groovy—taking each of us in briefly, and then he left.

Reuben immediately then took his position at the blackboard that was usually pushed against the wall. He and Sands began, and the rest of us very slowly joined in until Reuben had covered the blackboard with phrases, what they called patterns for the building—sloping roofs, alcoves, extended thresholds, hidden passageways, rays of light, soulful common areas, the weaving of light and dark, clustering rehearsal rooms, simple hearths, thick walls, a dance hall, radiant heat, filtered light, pools of light, arrows of darkness, secret doorways. . . .

I was already developing a rule never to look at Sands, in order not to give myself away and make her nervous. But there was something in her—some combination of joy and intelligence and seriousness—that seemed unrepeatable to me. Her voice had a vaguely foreign sound to it, a rough inflection left over from someplace in the world that I couldn't quite locate. Her clothes were as plain as possible and her hair pulled back in a ponytail, all as if she were trying to overcome beauty, but this would be like lashing down sails in a high wind. You might get a hand on one stretch, but then the rest would fly away, billowing out.

At one point Reuben and Sands got into an argument. Reuben suggested that the building ought to be cloaked in some sense of the spiritual.

"Reuben," Sands said. "I'm so tired of all our plans having to be so holy. It's such a dull way to think of buildings. And especially a theater."

Reuben looked a little amused. "Maybe we're going to have to divide up again," he said.

"Divide?" said Indira, who up until now had stayed silent. When she spoke, her earrings made tiny, almost imperceptible bell sounds.

"Last year," Sands said to her, "we had to divide into those who believe in God and those who don't."

"Just like that?" I said. "You know, people spend their whole lives on this question."

"It's just for now," Sands said. "I don't think He'll hold you to it." She already knew I'd be coming with her. And I did, risking hell for her, complaining all the way. The two of us worked in a tiny glass balcony, a little limb off of the commons. That first night Sands did most of the drawing, and I stood aside and made my suggestions, sometimes saying them more and more emphatically until she would finally draw them in. "Fine, fine," she'd say. We started over many times, a process that previously had seemed to me an indication of failure, but to Sands it was entirely normal, as if each building she called forth introduced her to other buildings it knew, and so working with her could be sort of an unwieldy process and you had to be willing to fight a little to get your way, but ultimately it was like walking into mysterious woods, everything related and fertile but constantly changing, and always there was the exhilarating feeling that one was continually losing and then finding the way.

More than anything, what I wanted was to enter into the rooms she drew, which would be like entering her imagination, that most private, far-flung place. By midnight we brought our draft to the others. It looked crazy, like big Russian circus tents connected by strings of light, like a big bohemian palace, but also very beautiful and somehow humble. I stood there while the others looked at it and felt as though I wanted to disown any participation in it whatsoever, and at the same time I was quite proud.

"It's so beautiful," Groovy said. Indira and Reuben nodded. And then they showed us theirs, which was austere and mysterious, rising out of the ground like it had just awoken and found itself the last thing on earth.

And we laid out the two buildings on the table and looked at them. They seemed so beautiful, as things can that are of the imagination. One had to love these figments, so exuberant in their postures and desires, trying to assert their way into the world.

"Yours is beautiful," Sands said, softly.

"*Yours* is," Groovy said. "God wouldn't even come to ours. He'd go to yours."

"Definitely He would go to yours," Sands said.

"If He existed," I said.

"Now He's really mad," Groovy said, and Sands laughed a little, putting her hand like a gentle claw on my elbow. I can feel to this day her hand where it gripped my elbow whenever she laughed. Each of her fingers sent a root system into my arm that traveled and traveled, winding and stretching and luxuriating throughout my body, settling there permanently.

THE NEXT MORNING ON our way to breakfast, Reuben and I saw Indira in the distance, making her way down the path to the river that wound about Fialta. There was already a rumor floating among us that Indira was a former Miss Bombay. I couldn't imagine this; she was so serious. She had a large poetry collection in her room and an eye for incredibly ornate, stylized design. Stadbakken had set her to work immediately on the gates and doorways for the theater. Watching her now, slipping down through the fall leaves, one could see the sadness and solitude that truly beautiful women inherit, which bears them quietly along. "Hey!" Reuben surprised me by calling out, and he veered away from me without even a glance back.

A WOMAN READING IS a grave temptation. I stood in the doorway separating the commons from our tiny kitchen, named Utopia for its sheer light and warmth, and hesitated for a long moment before I cleared my throat. Sands looked up. She was wearing glasses, her hair pulled back in a dark ponytail. She said hello.

"What're you reading?" I asked.

"Oh, this is Vitruvius—*The Ten Books of Architecture.* Stadbakken lent it to me."

"It's good?"

"I suppose. He's asked me to think about the threshold."

"The threshold. That's romantic."

She stared at me. Probably men were always trying to find an angle with her. Her face was beautiful, dark and high-hearted. "What do you mean by romantic?" she said.

This was really the last thing I wanted to define at this moment. It seemed any wrong answer and all my hopes might spiral up and away behind her eyes. "Well, I guess I mean romantic in the large sense, you know. The threshold is the moment one steps inside, out of the cold, and feels oneself treasured on a human scale."

"That's pretty," she said. She was eating Cheerios and toast.

"You know, I never found out the other night where you are from," I said.

"From? I am from Montreal originally."

"You went to McGill?"

"Laval," she said.

I knew Laval from pictures in architecture books. In my books it had looked like a series of dark, wintry ice palaces. "And how did you get from there to here?" I asked.

"Stadbakken came and gave a lecture. I met him there."

My mind was at once full of the image of her and Stadbakken in her tiny, cold Canadian room, its small space heater whirring out warmth, the animal skins on the floor and the bed, the two of them eating chipped beef from a can or whatever people eat in the cold, her mirror ringed with pictures of her young boyfriends — servicemen from across the border, maybe — and then of them clasped together, his age so incredible as it fell into her youth.

"Is he in love with you?" I asked.

"Not in love, no," she said. Which of course made me think that his feelings for her were nothing so simple or banal as love. It was far richer and more tangled in their psyches than that — some father/daughter, teacher/student, famous/struggling artist extravaganza that I could never comprehend.

And then Groovy approached, jangling her keys. Her hair had all these little stitched-people barrettes in it. It was bright blond, and the little primitive people all had panicked looks on their faces, as if they were escaping a great fire. "Stadbakken wants to see you," she said to Sands.

Sands started to collect her books and her tray, and Groovy turned to me. "I heard you're taking care of those cows," she said.

"Yes. And you?"

"Trash," Groovy said. "All the trash, every day, in every room."

"That's a big job. How about you?" I asked Sands.

"She's his favorite," Groovy said.

"So, no work then?" I asked.

"Oh, it's a lot of work, trust me," Groovy said, winking a little lewdly, and then Sands smiled at me a little, and then they both left me to my breakfast.

THERE WAS A CHAIR in one corner of the commons that was highly coveted. It had been designed by one of Stadbakken's former apprentices, and it was nearly the perfect chair for reading. That night I was just about to sit in it with my copy of Stadbakken's biography when Groovy came out of nowhere and hip-checked me. She sat down. She was reading Ovid.

"Chivalry's dead," I said, and sat in one of the lesser chairs across from her.

"On the contrary," she said, settling in. "I was helping you to be chivalrous."

"Well then, thank you."

She was sucking on a butterscotch candy that I could smell all the way from where I sat.

"How's that book?" she said.

"It's pretty interesting," I said. "Except the woman writing the book seems to have a real bone to pick with him. It's like the book's written by an ex-wife or something."

"Does he have ex-wives?"

"Four of them," I said.

"He's hard to love, I bet."

"I expect so. The book says he loves unrequited love, and once love is requited he seeks to make it unrequited."

"I see that a lot," Groovy said.

"Really?"

"Yeah, everybody loves a train in the distance."

Which is when Sands appeared. "Choo-choo," I said. Groovy smiled.

"What's up?" Sands asked. She stood behind Groovy, touching her hair, absently braiding it.

"He's lecturing me on unrequited love," Groovy said.

"What's his position?" Sands smiled at me. "Pro or con?"

"Very con," I said.

"Pro," Groovy said. "Look at him. It's obviously pro. It's practically carved in his forehead."

▼ ▼ ▼

FIALTA DID EXIST PRIOR to Stadbakken. It was originally a large house atop a rolling hill, in which a poet of some significance lived in the late nineteenth century. Apparently Walt Whitman, both Emerson and Thoreau, Jones Very, and even Herman Melville had passed through these walls during the years that America became what it is, when the individual stepped out of the light of its community and every life became, as Philip Larkin later said, a brilliant breaking of the bank. Stadbakken's father had been a member of this circle of friends and had bought the house from the poet in the year 1947; Stadbakken had grown up here as an only child. His parents had cherished him so fastidiously that he had no choice but to grow up to be, as his biographer put it, the ragingly immature man that he was, his inner child grown wild as the thorny vines that clung to the spruce down near the river.

Stadbakken went to school on the East Coast, lived for a while in New York City in his twenties, and then returned to Fialta and built his workshop here, presiding over it in his brimming room, up about a hundred turning wooden stairs, where I joined him every Tuesday afternoon at five. We would speak privately up here about my sketches, most of which involved Sands, about our plans for the theater, and also just about architecture in general. If you read about Stadbakken these days you will learn that as a teacher he can be offhand, blunt, manipulative, domineering, and arrogant, and though this is all true, his faults stood out in relief against the very lovely light of his generosity, like trees along a dimming horizon. He would turn his moony, moody eye on a sketch and see things I had never imagined — sunlit pools, fragrant winding gardens, gathering parties, cascading staircases. He would see people living out their lives. He would see life on earth. I would emerge from these sessions with him wanting desperately to run and run to catch up with his idea of what I might do, and in this way he created within me an ambition that would long outlast our association.

"WHAT I WAS THINKING," Sands was saying to me, while she leaned over our drafting table to turn on the bent-arm lamp, "was that we might bring the theater's balcony about two hundred and fifty degrees around. Wouldn't that be beautiful, and just a little strange?"

As she reached for the lamp, her body was crumpling up a map we had laid out of Chicago. "You're crumpling the map," I said.

"What?" She turned her face to me. It was riveting — dark and light in equal measure. Her skin had a kind of uneven quality to it that brought to mind childhood and all its imperfections, sun and dirt.

"Oh, nothing," I said. Would that the city be crumpled and destroyed by such a torso breaking over it — the Chicago River bursting its banks and running into the streets, the skyscrapers crashing down, the light extinguished suddenly by that gorgeous, obliterating darkness. We had until morning together to produce a plan that met a number of Stadbakken's and the client's specifications, which included these words—*bold, rich, witty,* and *wise.*

"It doesn't sound like a building," she said.

"I know, it sounds like my grandmother in the Bronx."

By the time we fell out, after finishing three reasonable drafts of interiors to show Stadbakken, it was nearly sunrise, and we went to Utopia, made ourselves cinnamon toast and coffee. I picked up the slop bucket that I set out on the kitchen floor every night with a sign above it for donations. This morning there was warm milk in which carrot shavings and potato peels and cereal and a lone Pop-Tart and some strips of cheese singles floated.

Sands accompanied me down through the field to the barn, which sat at the foot of the campus. We stood in the doorway as the shafts of sun fell through the high windows. The four cows were in their various stages—lying and dreaming and chewing and standing.

Sands stood quietly, peering at the cows. The standing cow looked back balefully.

"This one is Anna," I said. And then I introduced the rest—Ellen, Lidian, Marie. "Groovy named them for Stadbakken's former wives. She's been reading Ovid, where women are frequently turned into heifers when the men can no longer live with them, or without them."

"And now they're trapped down here forever."

"Punished for their beauty."

The cows lived so languorously from one day to the next that their being banished women seemed entirely possible. I was moving aside some hay so that I could set down the milking stool. I looked over to Sands, at her blackened form in the bright doorway. She moved then, and the sun unleashed itself fully into the barn. Daylight. For a moment Sands disappeared, but then coalesced again, this time sitting against the doorframe.

There was some silence as I struggled to elicit milk from the cow, a project that is part Zen patience, part desperate persuasion, and finally I did it. "Yay," Sands said softly. Some doves fluttered from their eaves and out the door.

"Stadbakken told me that if I wanted to build well, I should study the cows," I told her.

"What did he mean?" she asked.

"No idea."

We both stared for a moment.

"They have those short legs," I said. "Under such huge torsos."

"But good heads," she said. "They've got good, well-balanced heads on their shoulders."

"I suppose."

"Maybe he meant to make a building the way a cow would, if a cow could, not one that looks like a cow."

"So, like a barn then," I said. "Something nice."

"Maybe they're quite glamorous thinkers. Maybe something jeweled and spiritual, like a temple in India, or Turkey."

"Yes," I said. I shifted my chair to the next cow.

"Are cows monogamous?" she asked.

"Don't know, but I expect so."

"Why?"

"Look at them. They're so big and slow."

"Yes, and look at their eyes."

I patted the cow, and the cow responded by not caring. I looked over at Sands. The sun had risen high enough that it was no longer blinding me. She was slumped sleepily against the doorframe, with her feet kicked up against the other side. Clasped in the V of her body was Fialta rising in the near distance, steam rising from it, brimming over with its internal contradiction.

STADBAKKEN HAD IN HIS office an enormous telescope, one of those through which you can actually discern a little of the moon's surface, but instead it was pointed at the earth.

"May I?" I finally asked one October day.

"Please," he said, and I looked down through it at the river, at the waves breaking softly on the banks, which were made of autumn leaves.

"Your work has been getting better and better," he said, behind me.

"Thank you."

"These beams are good. Where did they come from?" He was pointing at one of my drawings.

This was sometimes hard to do, to trace where elements came from in a sketch. It was not unlike pulling apart images from a dream.

"I guess from the barn," I said, which was true, though I hadn't realized it until now.

"Of course," he said. "I saw you walking down there today. How's that going, by the way? How are the cows?"

He must have seen me, trudging in my sleep through the dark field? It made me a little nervous, and anyway the question seemed doubly intimate, since I half believed the cows really were his banished wives. "They're doing well," I said.

"Let me show you something," he said. And from a long drawer he pulled out a series of drawings of Fialta. I had never seen any of his sketches before. It was almost impossible to read them, the lines were so thin and reedy, and they seemed all out of proportion to me, so that Fialta looked like it was blowing in the wind, or maybe going up in flames. He slid out the plan for the barn and laid it out in front of us. "Here she is," he said. "I built it in 1967."

"The summer of love, sir."

"Yes, it was."

One of the things Stadbakken had been struggling to

teach us that fall was that a building ought to express two things simultaneously. The first was permanence, that is, security and well-being, a sense that the building will endure through all sorts of weather and calamity. But it also ought to express an understanding of its mortality, that is, a sense that it is an individual and, as such, vulnerable to its own passing away from this earth. Buildings that don't manage this second quality cannot properly be called architecture, he insisted. Even the simplest buildings, he said, ought to be productions of the imagination that attempt to describe and define life on earth, which of course is an overwhelming mix of stability and desire, fulfillment and longing, time and eternity.

The barn, even in this faint sketch, revealed this. It knew. "It's beautiful, sir," I said.

"Thank you," he said.

It seemed only right, I thought, as I spiraled down into the evening air alone, that the cows had such a place to live, since they themselves seemed hybrids of this earth and the next, animals and angels both.

THE TRADITION, REUBEN informed us, was that apprentices put on a show for Stadbakken. At first we were going to do a talent show, but nobody could drum up a talent. And then we were going to write skits, but they all ended up involving each of us doing bad impressions of him. And then we landed on the idea of putting on a play. He could be in it, too. We'd give him a part to read at the performance, which was to take place at Thanksgiving. We decided first to do *King Lear,* and then *Measure for Measure,* and then Beckett, and then *Arcadia,* and ruled all of these out as we started to cast them. Finally, Reuben suggested *Angels in America.*

"There's no women in it," Sands said, when Reuben suggested it.

"There's gay men," I said to her, "and one woman."

"Gay men are not the equivalent of women."

"Stadbakken likes women better than men," Groovy said.

"Everybody does," Sands said.

I frowned. "So rude," I said to her.

Still, we decided to do *Angels,* with women playing the parts of the gay men, and then, through some hysterical fair play, I ended up with the part of the woman. Indira would be the angel, hovering above gender, and *sodo-sudu* entirely.

IF YOU DID WANT to know what Stadbakken believed about women, all you had to do was step into the women's wing at Fialta, with its great, circular common room. There were no walls at all. We were all sitting around the enormous wooden table at the room's center. We were drinking sugar gin, and from here it was as if the room seemed to believe that women were so in love with other women that they needed no walls at all. Probably when there were no men in the room they passed right through each other as well.

"What was that you read me from Vitruvius?" I asked Sands. "That the walls of his Utopia were made of respect and interest only?"

"So much for a room of her own," Sands said.

"My therapist would be appalled at this room," Groovy said.

"You have a therapist?" I asked. "Where is he, out in the woods?"

"He's a little gnome."

"You sit on his mushroom, talk about your boundary problems," I said.

"You think I have boundary problems?" she said.

I had been joking, but now that the question was put to me, I foolishly answered it. "Well, a little, I guess."

Sands looked at me, horrified.

"In a good way," I said. "It's charming."

"I think you have boundary problems," Groovy said. "There's such a thing as too-strict boundaries, you know. You're all cut off from everybody."

"I am?" I felt just the opposite. I felt like I bled all over everything, in an unseemly fashion, and my feelings for Sands were exacerbating this.

The conversation continued, with allegations and

drunken accusations, all led by Groovy and me, the two most insecure parties in the group. Finally the phone rang for Indira, and she stepped into the kitchen to speak. None of us could understand the language, but her voice became louder and more upset as the conversation progressed.

Groovy brought out the cake she'd made for us, an Ovid cake. "It has in it all the foods mentioned in the *Metamorphoses*—cranberries, walnuts, cinnamon, cloves," she said.

"There are marshmallows in Ovid?" I asked, after I took a bite.

"Oh, those," Groovy said. "Those are my signature."

"She puts marshmallows in everything," Sands said. And then Indira returned to the room, apologizing as she sat down. "I'm supposed to be getting married in two months."

"What?" we all said.

"Yes. But I don't want to."

Reuben looked stricken. "It's an arranged marriage?" he said.

"Well, sort of."

"Who arranged it?"

"I did, actually. But it was four years ago, before I went to Princeton and my fiancé to Penn. We planned to return to Bombay and get married, but I fell out of touch with him. Meanwhile, our fathers have joined businesses, and everybody awaits my arrival."

We talked about this for a while and tried to strategize

ways out. By the time midnight rolled around, Sands caught up to me in the kitchen and suggested we peel away, go to the river.

AND WHAT IS A love affair if not a little boat, pushing off from shore, its tilting, untethered bob, its sensitivity to one's quietest gestures?

"I would love an arranged marriage," Sands said. I was pushing us away from the edge with my oar, breaking apart the thin skein of ice forming there.

"No you wouldn't."

"Yes. I'd like to have a family so involved that they were planning the wedding and I just had to show up, the treasured bride." And then she rose in the boat, and as she stood it was as if the world shifted off course and was just careening back and forth, drunkenly. The trees shook with interest. She stretched and yawned, lifting her arms. Her sweater lifted, so that a narrow strip of her stomach showed. It was like burnished wood, pierced with a ruby. She looked almost psychedelically pretty there, in the tunnel created by the trees over the river.

I would have kissed her then, struggled up through the ranks of myself to do this one true thing, except I made the mistake of glancing up first, through the ragged arms of trees. And there was Stadbakken's room alight. A cold wind reared suddenly, and I could feel minuscule shards of ice embedded in it. By the time the river froze, we would no longer be together, and I could feel in the air already the terrible possibility.

THE NEXT AFTERNOON, HOW could I help but think he had seen us, through his telescope, since when I entered for my tutorial, the first thing he did was lift my sketches to the light and say, "I don't think you and Sands are working well together at all anymore."

"Why?"

"I used to see Sands all over the page, and now I don't see her here at all."

I didn't think this was fair, nor particularly true. "Maybe our work is starting to become similar."

"Oh." He looked at me sarcastically. "The two become one then, is that it?" He actually leaned up against the telescope then. If either of us had looked through it, probably we would have seen the river shrinking, crackling, crystallizing itself into ice.

WE HAD ONE REHEARSAL, a run-through in the commons. Reuben was the director. Stadbakken was going to be given the most expansive part in the play, the part of the dying Prior. And Indira was the angel, of course. Sands had made wings. If I hadn't loved Sands before the wings, I would have now, for they were made of the feathers and down of creatures that had to be imaginary—white and brown and long. Picture her in the dewy morning coming off the hill to wrestle down a figment, tear off its feathers, later affixing them with glue to bent clothes hangers and panty hose straps, and there you have Sands and everything about her.

Sands and Groovy played the parts of Louie and Joe, respectively, two gay men. Their interpretations of men were hilarious—strangely deep throated and spliced through with their ideas of gayness, which were like streams of joy running through.

I played a luminous, heartbroken, and uptight woman whom Joe had abandoned. I took her husband's rejection of her quite seriously, tried to imagine exactly how it would feel as I swished in my housecoat along the floor of the commons.

After the rehearsal, I was sitting in the sheepskin chair, minding my own business, when Sands and Groovy came along to deliver their verdict on my performance. "You don't really have being a woman quite right," Sands said.

"What do you mean?"

"Well, you need to feel it inside."

"I can feel it inside," I said.

"You looked kinda stiff."

"No, I didn't. That was my interpretation."

"You gotta loosen up." Sands reached down to shake my shoulders a little.

"You do," I said, and I reached for her, and I brought her to me. Her body was such a mysterious rolling landscape in those moments, it turned and turned and turned, and I could feel her falling into my lap. I don't know what I would have done then, some minor consummation of my feelings for her, but Stadbakken stepped into the room. It was very odd to see him in daylight. Sands stood up, not too quickly, but definitely a little shaken.

"Where is Indira?" he said. "Her father has called me."

"I'll find her," I said. I thought she might be back in the room with Reuben, and I knew he would be mortified if Stadbakken knew this.

And I did find them there, sitting across from each other at Reuben's folding table, two beautiful solitudes greeting each other across a little distance, playing cards.

I THINK IT WOULD have been possible to maintain this little world, always on the edge of fruition, if we hadn't spent Thanksgiving together, hours on hours together, if we hadn't consumed so much sugar gin, if we hadn't put on such a beautiful play. It was a snowy day. Dinner was planned for nightfall, which was five p.m. in these parts. Stadbakken would be arriving at four-thirty, at the dimming of the day. So we all met to cook in Utopia at one, after a morning of working alone on our sketches of the theater.

For the first hour we mostly drank. Sands enforced a game of Monopoly, and then we began to cook. Groovy made little pancake hors d'oeuvres, studded with cloves and cinnamon. Reuben and I were in charge of the turkey and the ham and the smaller game hens. Indira was in and out, miraculously cooking gorgeous yams and some exotic bean dish at the same time she was dissolving a multimillion-dollar marriage deal in Bombay on her cell without even breaking a sweat. She just kept rearranging things with her long, bronze hands, which I guess is what cooking is.

Sands relaxed in the commons, reading a book. She had been to town early in the morning to get the drinks and seemed to believe this exempted her from any further participation in the meal, except for leaning against the doorjamb every now and then to read us a passage from her novel, which today was *Justine,* by Lawrence Durrell: "Certainly she was bad in many ways, but they were all small ways. Nor can I say she harmed nobody. But those she harmed most she made fruitful. She expelled people from their old selves."

"That's you, all right," I said.

"It's me, too," Groovy said.

"It's totally you," Sands said, complimenting her.

I was trying to break open the plastic surrounding the turkey, surprised and humbled by all the blood that poured out as it opened. "How does anybody eat after they've cooked a meal?" I said.

"Welcome to being a woman," Sands said.

"Well," I said, "we have to kill them. That's hard work."

"Nobody killed that," she said. "It wasn't ever really alive."

"It was," I said, newly in touch with animals from my months in the barn. I held out the turkey a little. "It had its days in the sun."

Sands smiled at me for a few long moments in which I arranged our whole future. We would live out our long chain of days at Fialta, secretly but not so secretly in love, and then we would move together to Chicago, or New York City, and live in our own private warren of rooms together. And our life would be made up of the gentle separations and communion of marriage. A line from a book Indira had given to Reuben ran through my mind, a sad line, I realize now, but it didn't even occur to me then that it was. "It was good to be alive when you were alive." My dream, as I stared at Sands, was crosshatched by our friends — Groovy, Indira, Reuben — moving back and forth between us, carrying on.

So, finally, the table was set, and the beloved guest had arrived, exuberant and windswept. He lifted his cup to us, and we drank, our bodies growing warmer as the day grew colder outside, whiter and whiter. The table was laid with the creatures, all burnished a coppery gold. And in the fireplace the log, like another little beast at work on itself, turned and turned as the air filled with the smell of fire. We lifted our cups back to Stadbakken. If you have ever felt that the table at which you sit contains everything and everybody that matters to you, like a little boat, then you know how I felt. It doesn't feel secure at all, but rather a little tipsy. It is unnerving to love a single place so much. There are no anchors to the world outside, the cities in the distance, the country around you. There is just this: the six of you afloat so happily in the temporary day.

AFTER DINNER, WE CLEARED away the dishes and then set about the scene from the play. "Okay," Sands said to Stadbakken, "you have a part." She handed him a Xeroxed copy of the play. "This chair you're sitting in? It's your bed. You're dying." She touched his shoulder when she told him this. My eyes settled on her hand, on his shoulder. And his eyes settled on my eyes.

And then the play began. Reuben narrated to Stadbakken what came before: love, disappointment, the crude beautiful drama of sex, Sands and Groovy vamping at love, Sands carrying on like a girl making fun of a boy making fun of a girl, with a painted mustache. She was so ridiculous and beautiful, I thought I might die. Beyond the play, the day darkened. The backdrop was the icy arms of trees, the lift of starlings against the falling sun, the day dying. When Indira's part came, we had to shout for her. She was in Utopia, arguing on her cell. She hung up the phone and came in. She began to cry as she delivered her line, which gave her part a weird veracity: "Heaven is a city much like San Francisco—more beautiful because imperiled." We carried on for a few seconds, but then realized she actually was crying, standing there.

"What's the matter?" Sands asked.

"My father, he's sick. They just told me. I have to leave tomorrow."

"Oh no!" Groovy said. And we all murmured. I looked over at Reuben. *What will you do now, Reuben? What display now? What will spill out of you now?* He stood so still, as the heartbroken always do, and then he went to her. He touched her wing, the safest, least intrusive part.

"Let's continue," Indira said.

And so we did.

"Since you believe the world is perfectible you find it always unsatisfying." This was Sands, as Louis. And then she kissed Groovy, as Joe. They kissed, as men kiss. I staggered inwardly. And the play wound through its tragedies easily until Stadbakken's final, deathbed lines. "You are all fabulous creatures, each and every one. And I bless you: More life." Behind his head thousands of birds took flight. He raised his arms, though dying. He loved the play, you could tell. The wind howled. And then he stood up to go hug Indira.

SINCE SANDS HADN'T COOKED, it was her duty to clean up. I helped her clear away the dishes. We made an enormous pile of dirty dishes and plates and heaps of food on the silver table at the center of Utopia. There were also the three empty carriages of bones. "I can't believe that about Indira," Sands said.

"I know. It's hard to believe."

"And now she'll have to get married. That's a real primal fear, you know, for women. I can remember as a girl having dreams about having to get married."

"You're so unromantic, I can't even stand it."

"Me?" she said.

"You."

She was leaning against the silver table, looking down at the turkey drumstick that she was tearing apart in her hands, to eat, when I stepped up, finally, and against all better reason, kissed her. Tomorrow, Indira would be gone, and who could predict what would happen then, when one of us was gone? Time was ticking away, the snow was falling. Sands's mouth tasted like ten thousand things—berries and wine and pumpkin and something too human to define. I placed my hand on her spine as it arched back over the table, and then the door swung open. I turned to see Stadbakken, my arm lifting Sands so that we stood before him, my arm around her. He was smoking a cigar, and some of its smoke was spiraling up around his head. He stood still for a moment and then said, "Oh, is that right? Well, then. Okay. That's fine."

He walked toward us then. "First, let's clear away the bones," he said. "Let's make some room, then, for you two. Let us clear away the bones!" And with that, he swept his

entire arm over the silver lake of the table, so that everything flew—all the bodies breaking up in the air, a flurry
of bone and gristle, of life sailing apart.

LATER THAT NIGHT I went looking for Sands. She
had kissed me, told me to wait in Utopia, and ran after
Stadbakken. "I'll try to solve it," she said to me. But then
she did not come back for over an hour. I went to the wom-
en's wing and found Groovy there, helping Indira to pack.
And then Reuben came out of Indira's room as well, carrying an empty cardboard box. He wasn't saying anything,
so I blurted, "Indira, why are you going? Please don't go.
Please stay."

Indira looked at me sweetly, indulgently, as if I were a
small child. She hugged me.

And then I went to Stadbakken's. The light was falling
down out of the building, onto the snow, that's how bright
it was. It was too high for me to see anything, but I stood
out in the snow for a long time. I must have stood there
for close to an hour. It was ridiculous, I knew, and pathetic,
but that light was more warm and significant than any I'd
ever known in my life, and I knew that when I turned to go
there would be nothing, only the cold and the never-ending
drifts of snow.

BY THE NEXT MORNING, our dinner was dissolving
in the slop bucket—the little pancakes, the heads of fish,

the turkey breast, the potato shavings. I poured a cup of coffee, picked up the pail, and walked down through the snow and darkness. The beasts were still asleep, and one startled when I opened the door and the cold sun fell over her. Eventually the snow began to fall—enormous lotus flakes that I watched from inside the barn. I milked the one cow for a while and as the sun rose higher I was finally getting warm. The barn was waking up around me, the building itself shifting and ticking away as the light forced itself through the million tiny chinks. As I milked I tried to think of a way to stay in love with Sands and stay at Fialta. In the moment Stadbakken flung his hand across the table, I had known he would never be reconciled to this. I don't believe there was anything illicit particularly in his feelings; in fact, it was probably their very purity that made them so searing, so intolerant. He was her teacher, and she his student, and they met up there in a perfect illumination high above the regular world. Another cow shuddered awake beside me and looked up at me, half in sympathy, half in resignation to all my shortcomings, which is the very look cows always give, which is their whole take on the world.

And then the door opened. The cold, dim day rushed in, and, along with it, Sands. She was wearing a nightgown with a parka over the top, her hair in one long, sleepy braid. She looked like she was fulfilling and making fun of my dreams all at once. "You look like a farmer's wife," I said.

"And you the farmer."

"He wants to see you," she said. Some doves in the rafters fluttered and made a break for the open door, wheeling then around the corner. Fialta was burning away in the distance. From this distance, it looked already to be stirring—composed, as Auden said all living things were, of dust and Eros. It was clear what would happen. I would leave; Stadbakken would fall—the full, staggering weight of him—in my arms and hug me as he told me I had to leave. But there was still the morning. Her hair and skin were the only moments of darkness in the brightening barn. I kissed her again. One of the cows made a lowing sound I'd not heard before, which sounded like a foghorn in the distance. They'd seen it all before, this whole drama; their large hearts inside them had broken a hundred times before today. The barn smelled exactly like the very passage of time. The cows took their own fertility so practically, as the pigs did joyfully, and the doves beautifully. I already knew then that I'd be forced to leave Fialta; I could practically have predicted my leaving to the hour, but my heart was caught up in the present, whirring away and still insisting that this was the beginning, not the end. And so that's how I felt hardly any grief at all, lying alongside Sands on the crackling, warm hay at the foot of that makeshift paradise, as the cows watched on, remembering human love.

SETTLERS

▼ ▼ ▼

This old house, belonging to my friends Lesley and
Andy, had been built in 1904 in a neighborhood that
pretended it was on solid ground — old, Victorian homes
with pillars and porticoes — but if you stepped through the
screen door into the garden out back, you could feel the
sand under your feet, and despite Lesley's beautiful mazes
of trees, you could tell the ocean had been here not long
ago, and would be again.

Lesley and I were the same age — both thirty-five — but
already she had three little girls, whom she was home-
schooling. I was standing at the big kitchen window and I
could see them out there in a corner of the garden, sitting in
a little circle with their babysitter, one by one racing around

and around, playing duck duck goose. There was a tropical storm on its way that evening, and it was already quite windy, and the girls' hair, all curly and brown, was flying around in the shifty air. It was such an ideal little world, and it seemed a wonder that Lesley had somehow generated it all—the house, the girls, the man, the stone pathways out back that made a labyrinth through the garden, the exquisite homemade dollhouses in every room of the house, made out of scraps of fabric and old cereal boxes, the batik banner hanging above this big window that said, A FAMILY LIKE NO OTHER.

Lesley and Andy were both originally from New York, both great conversationalists—full of curiosity and insight. They were both busily cooking tonight—Andy a kind of dark, sticky roast, and Lesley her specialty— a Vietnamese pho soup. If a person could measure these things, I'd say she had the upper hand in the relationship, but not by too much, just a little, just enough to offset what feminists used to call the "slide toward male dominance" in the culture at large and create a perfectly symmetrical, very powerful little system within a system, a neat counterbalance. I used to think of them as a "productive" couple, meaning their marriage seemed to give them energy rather than drain it away.

David Booth was already there, standing in a corner of the kitchen, with a bottle of beer in his hand. He was the perfect man—calm, intelligent, nice—though it didn't ever seem to dawn on him—ever—no matter how many situations he and I found ourselves in that duplicated a date—at our mutual friends' home for dinner, for instance, or at a carnival with a group of friends, all couples except for us, or walking across campus at *dusk,* the perfume of huge and strange southern flowers all around us—that the two of us could try to date. Would it kill us?

It was September 11, 1998, which was the day the Starr Report had emerged in the newspapers. All of us had spent the day poring over it. I was working on a TV pilot and was supposed to be writing revisions, but instead I'd spent the day with the *New York Times* laid out on my desk as I read it—rapt, nearly unconscious. It was seventy-four pages long, and the writer had been good enough to write it as a narrative, complete with suspense, structure, style, and substance. It was like reading Edith Wharton, minus all the fussy details. Lesley and I had been calling each other all day, on and off, to discuss it. "I don't know," I said now to her, "I just really emerged with the feeling that Clinton hadn't really wanted to betray Hillary at all. In my reading, I thought he was trying to *resist* temptation the whole time."

"Oh please," Lesley said. "It's as if we read entirely different documents. He originates most of the action."

"But only after he resists quite a few times. And he mentions Hillary many times. She is on his mind!"

David Booth lifted his beer in a little toast at this, which I thought was charming.

"Oh spare me my husband ever uttering my name while he's having an affair," Lesley said. She had already spooned out the soup into the bowls and now was carrying them, two by two, into the dining room.

"Noted," Andy said.

"I'd want to be on his mind," I said. "That smells amazing." Just the fact that it was real food seemed miraculous to me, after a day of drinking only coffee and eating M&M's. Somehow Lesley had found the rabbit hole into real life, while I had continued on this other precarious path—single and free and mostly what I wanted, but still, there wasn't any real food, it seemed, no soups or stews or casseroles, except for the two or three nights a month when I came to dinner here.

"How's that TV pilot coming?" David Booth asked me, as we all sat down to eat. One of us was missing—Berber— but she was always late. She always came flying in, with a great excuse. I was quite anxious to see her since apparently she had just made a decision, reported to Lesley earlier in the week, to abandon her life amongst us and go "join with" a man—a married man—she had met at a yoga retreat in the mountains. Lesley had also warned me she was wearing a turban these days, and I wanted to see that, too.

"It's coming terribly, honestly," I said to David Booth. "My writing partner and I can't agree on anything, and there are fifty other people with all sorts of opinions, and nobody agrees. It's all a big mess."

"It's about Wonder Woman still?" he asked.

David Booth had written and published a book last year called *The Continuing City*, a book of essays that was so beautiful and thrilling it made me nervous to read it. Every essay—whether it was about reading Voltaire in boarding school, or his mother's career as a film actress in the sixties, or his grandmother's recipe for lamb—always wound its way into some really beautiful reckoning with fate, and life, and God. So I didn't like it that he described my project as a TV pilot about Wonder Woman, even thought that's exactly what it was.

"It is," I said.

"What are her powers anyway?" Andy asked. "I should know that."

"She can force men to tell the truth," I said. "She has a lasso that can do that."

"She has an invisible airplane," Lesley said.

"One thing about her," I said, "that often gets lost in all the scripts is that she can love unconditionally. She can love people who don't love her back."

"That's a *superpower*?" Andy said.

"No mortal can do it," I said.

Which is when Berber appeared, bringing in the deep green verdant smell of their front lawn, as well as the ocean. The turban made her look a number of conflicting things—pure and spiritual for sure, but also completely cracked in the head, like she'd had an actual surgical procedure, or maybe an imaginary one. But then it also somehow emphasized her big, square, beautiful teeth.

"Berber, we've started," Lesley said. "I'm sorry. We didn't know if you'd make it."

"Oh that's fine," Berber said, and quickly slid into her chair.

"We've been talking about the Starr Report. Did you read it?" asked Lesley.

"I would have slept with him, of course I would have."

"Is this how women think?" Andy said.

"What do you mean?" I said.

"Well, I thought you'd all be censorious of him, but really what you're doing is thinking about whether you would sleep with him or not."

"You can have both those thoughts at the same time," I said. "You can feel very critical of a man even as you're sleeping with him," I said. David Booth laughed a little at this, a gesture that was enough to keep me interested in him for another few years.

"That explains a lot," Andy said.

"What about this guy?" I said to Berber. "What's going on?"

"Lesley told you then. He's wonderful."

"Is there going to be a ceremony or something?"

"We haven't worked out the details, but yes."

"So he's getting a divorce?"

"No, his wife is very sick. She's in a home."

"She's dying," David Booth said.

"She is."

"Have you met her or something?" I said.

"Yes. She wants Bryan and me to be together."

Later that night, David and I left the party together. He walked me to my car. The eastern seaboard at night in September is so beautiful, so warm and cold, and the streetlights threw such bright light on the street that it was almost like a movie set. "What do you think?" I said, "About this Bryan person?"

"Yeah, it's interesting, isn't it? I don't know. I've been reading about a Utopian community from the late 1800s, in Massachusetts, called Fruitlands. I had the same feeling while listening to Berber's set up. This should work, but I know it won't. How can it?"

BY THE TIME WE met Bryan, it was a few months later, in December, at Lesley and Andy's annual Christmas party. I was there with David Booth. He had even picked me up in his little car. Looking back, this was the night I silently broke up with him, even though we weren't dating. The house looked magnificent; Lesley and the girls had draped piney garlands everywhere, and even just the smell of pine and cinnamon was suggestive of the deepest, richest kind of family life. How could David not want this for the two of us—a big fire, our homeschooled children circulating with little silver trays of food, and then the inevitable long gossipy discussions after everyone left and we languidly picked up the living room and then settled down on the couch together.

It was easy to spot Berber and Bryan, since they both were wearing their turbans, which as far as I was concerned joined them more absolutely than marriage.

Bryan reached out immediately to shake my hand. He recognized me without an introduction. He had one of those broad, merry, twinkly faces, with a gap in his teeth. He just looked happy. He looked so happy you wanted to make him more happy. "It's so nice to meet you," he said warmly. "I've heard so much about you. Berber just loves you so much," he said.

"Oh thank you!" I said. "I love her. And this is David Booth."

And here Bryan bowed slightly. "David Booth," he said in a low, dramatic voice. "Your book was the work of a genius."

"Thank you," David said. "Thank you for reading it."

"The essay on *Tommy* alone was worth the price of admission."

"Oh, thank you." (One had to say thank you continually to Bryan; every conversation was engineered that way.) "Yeah, *Tommy*," David went on, "I saw that when I was eight, perhaps the most impressionable age possible. And then my older brothers played the Who till late in the night, every night, in the basement, so those lyrics are just permanent background in my brain."

Bryan pantomimed an air guitar and sang in an actually really pretty falsetto, "Deaf, dumb, and blind kid, sure plays mean pinball."

Berber smiled and nodded a little. She seemed so charmed by him, and I was, too, still, at this point. His cup was full to the brim, and just a little over.

"And how's Wonder Woman?" Berber asked me, a little conspiratorially.

"She's good," I said.

"It's a movie script?" Bryan asked.

"TV," I said.

"TV," Bryan said. "I barely know what's on TV these days. I like what you said, David, in one of your essays about TV, that it replaces experience to such an extent that the person is no longer privy to the great truths that lie at the heart of action."

Oh, this. "Well, what about *Tommy*? *Tommy* doesn't do that somehow? Cause it was on a bigger screen?"

"Oh," David said, "and I was just posturing. Some of those essays are just bullshit. You know, you get writing, and you just try out ideas."

"At our yoga retreat—where we met—there are no screens of any sort allowed and what we've found is that people have access to the deeper stories of their lives when you're not distracting them with the shallow, irrelevant stories from a television. Berber and I, for instance, both have shadowy ideas of knowing each other in the past."

"Really?" I looked at Berber. She sort of shrugged. She was a little embarrassed, I could tell.

"Yes," he said. "We think we were married in the past. During a plague. One of us perished. I mean, who knows, right? It can't be known, but we both felt a strong connection to the past when we met."

"And your wife, who was she in this scenario?" And then I instantly regretted it, because a look of such absolute sadness passed over his face.

"I guess nothing is simple," he said.

DAVID AND I REALLY did break up, even though he was unaware of it. But without me calling all the time, we never saw each other, except here and there, once or twice a year, by accident. And in the meantime I got married to an old friend named Mark. He ran the Raptor Center in our town, in the black swamps to the west of us, alongside the Cape Fear River. If you looked carefully, he was a wonderful man. He played the harmonica, he had a beard, he was ten years older than me, he was a settled man, and smart and humble, you could trust him never to have an affair or even leave the house too much. I got pregnant right away, which we'd planned. He was not here tonight. He told me to go ahead, that he'd already had dinner at Lesley and Andy's, as if dinner with friends were one of those things you did once, to experience it, and never again.

It was 2005, and Lesley and Andy's home had undergone

some major changes. About five years earlier Lesley had discovered a series of pointless affairs Andy had partici- pated in thoughout their marriage, nothing too serious but of course completely devastating to Lesley. Her solution was not to leave him, but to add all sorts of extra rooms and dividers into their home, as if to demarcate places for herself and places for him, and then some mutual territories as well. She'd also installed a huge flat-screen TV high on their kitchen wall. Tonight it showed Hurricane Katrina bearing down on New Orleans. The sound was off but the mesmerizing scenes of water pouring down city streets were both beautiful and terrible to look at.

Berber and Bryan were standing under the television, newly married and with their turbans off, thankfully. Bryan had cornered David and was asking him about his newest book. "Are we meant to believe that there is or isn't a God by the end?"

This made David laugh. "I really don't know," he said, as he hugged me hello.

Lesley and David had lined up two lasagnas end to end— she had made one vegetarian and he had made one meat, and they lay there under the candlelight, awaiting us. I was so hungry. I'd been so sad for the last two weeks that I hadn't been able to eat. I was in the middle of a protracted miscarriage—the baby still alive, but with a heartbeat mea- suring once a minute, like one of those sea creatures that live at the floor of the ocean.

"I saw it," David said to me. "I saw the show."

"Oh yeah?" I said. "What'd you think?"

"I thought it was great," he said. "I really did. All that derring-do. And the culture is ready for a big dose of feminism."

"You think?"

"Yes. If I were a woman, I'd want to be an Amazon."

"Thanks," I said. And then he touched my arm, just like that, which so surprised me that I nearly fell into his arm. It must be exactly what men don't want—you reach to touch a woman lightly and then she falls into you, her whole weight, which in this case included another man's dying baby. "Sorry!" I said. Sorry to David Booth for falling into him, and sorry to baby, for everything. For no life.

But anyway, life isn't that good always. I wished I could let the baby know that. There's a lot that's lousy. It's true there are large turning structures—Ferris wheels—that will carry people high into the air above the ocean, that is true, and then around the next corner there are funhouses, those are great, and then there are just ordinary playgrounds on every corner, and there are things not even for children that are for children, like church spires that look like weather vanes, and there is one downtown that actually spins, a little spinning cross, an image that would live in the child's mind maybe forever, gathering ideas to it, spinning madly but also stable there, and in tonight's wind it wouldn't even be a cross, it would be distorted into

maybe a little question mark, and standing for all the children in town as a kind of fervent lasting joyful little thing
they always know. So there is a lot, admittedly.

But then you grow up and you get a wonderful man
and he cheats on you, or you get somebody like Bryan,
who at your wedding says this as his vow—"I will be your
teacher and you will be my team." Or you get David Booth,
in which case you marry somebody else.

We sat down to the his and hers lasagnas, right as the
last levees were breached and the ninth ward completely
overwhelmed. See, I said to the baby, look at the seawater
rising, look at the cats and dogs on the roof, it's okay to just
pass along, *(I will miss you!)*, just keep going.

ACKNOWLEDGMENTS

This book was written with thanks to (but not about) my family: Don and Marilyn Lee, Emma Beke and Stephen Beke, Wendy Arnold, Steve Arnold, Joshua Arnold, Jessica Arnold, Eric Lee, Janya Wongsopa, John Beke, Allison Beke, Paul Beke, Alexander Bilson, and Kate Bilson.

Many thanks to writers and friends in Wilmington: Dana Sachs, Todd Berliner, Karen Bender, Robert Siegel, Nina de Gramont, David Gessner, Philip Gerard, Phil Furia, Jill Gerard, Mark Cox, Malena Morling, Sarah Messer, Michael White (*Picture me floating down through the fires of this day and the next*), John Sullivan, Mariana Johnson, Hannah Abrams, Kimi Faxon Hemingway, Emily Smith, Ben George, Tim Bass, Lavonne Adams, Clyde Edgerton, Kristina Edgerton, Virginia Holman, Megan Hubbard, Beau Bishop, Lisa Bertini, Peter Trachtenberg, and Wendy

Brenner, who routinely says lines so funny that I try to immediately put them into stories, plagiarism that she cheerfully tolerates.

Many thanks also to C. Michael Curtis, Sumanth Prabhaker, Adrienne Brodeur, Nicole Winstanley, and Leslie Bienen.

And also, to Doug Stewart, who is the best, fastest, nicest, and smartest agent in the world.

And to everyone at Algonquin, huge thanks: Elisabeth Scharlatt, Ina Stern, Brunson Hoole, Anne Winslow, Kelly Bowen, Debra Linn, Emma Boyer, Chuck Adams, Lauren Moseley, Katie Ford, Craig Popelars. And thank you to Kathy Pories, whose thinking is poised perfectly, at every moment, between serious and funny.